PYGMY

By the same author

CHUCK
PALAHNIUK
PYGMY

Jonathan Cape
London

Published by Jonathan Cape 2009

2 4 6 8 10 9 7 5 3 1

Copyright © Chuck Palahniuk 2009

Chuck Palahniuk has asserted his right under the Copyright, Designs
and Patents Act, 1988 to be identified as the author of this work

First published in Great Britain in 2009 by
Jonathan Cape
Random House, 20 Vauxhall Bridge Road,
London SW1V 2SA

www.rbooks.co.uk

Addresses for companies within The Random House Group Limited can be
found at: www.randomhouse.co.uk/offices.htm

The Random House Group Limited Reg. No. 954009

A CIP catalogue record for this book
is available from the British Library

ISBN 9780224087131 (Hardback edition)
ISBN 9780224087148 (Trade paperback edition)

The Random House Group Limited supports The Forest Stewardship
Council (FSC), the leading international forest certification organisation.
All our titles that are printed on Greenpeace approved FSC certified paper
carry the FSC logo. Our paper procurement policy can be found at:
www.rbooks.co.uk/environment

Printed and bound in the UK by
CPI Mackays, Chatham ME5 8TD

To Amy Hempel—
—There is no other cheese.

He alone, who owns the youth, gains the future.

—*Adolf Hitler*

PYGMY

Dispatch
First

Begins here first account of operative me, agent number 67, on arrival Midwestern American airport greater ███████ area. Flight ███████. Date ███████. Priority mission top success to complete. Code name: Operation Havoc.

Fellow operatives already pass immigrant control, exit through secure doors and to embrace own other host family people. Operative Tibor, agent 23; operative Magda, agent 36; operative Ling, agent 19. All violate United States secure port of entry having success. Each now embedded among middle-income corrupt American family, all other homes, other schools and neighbors of same city. By not after next today, strategy web of operatives to be established.

Passport man, officer nothing behind bullet glass, open and reading passport book of operative me, matching to paper facts of visa, man down look upon this agent, say, "You're a long ways from home, son." Man, ancient penned animal dying of too tall, pooled heavy blood hanging in leg veins. Trapped all day, then could be next walk to toilet, *pow-pow*, clot knock out brain.

Passport man say, "So, you're an exchange student?" Man say, "How old are you, my boy?"

On fingers of operative me, am to count one, two until thirteen.

"So you're thirteen?" say passport man. Behind glass, say, "Awful small for your age, aren't you?"

Operative me say, One-three. Hold fingers straight and say repeat, Thirteen.

Iron fist of operative me, could be, flash fire explode, *powbang*. Burst bullet glass. Striking Cobra Quick Kill maneuver so collapse passport man windpipe. Render instant quick dead.

Tongue of operative me lick, licking, touching back tooth on bottom, molar where planted inside forms cyanide hollow, touching not biting. Not yet. Tooth wet smooth against lick of tongue. Swallow spit, say counting one, two, counting on fingers of hand until six. Tell passport man, to be exchange student with host family six month.

Passport man strike paper of book with ink, marked good to enter nation. Slide passport book returned to this agent. Man say, "Welcome to the greatest country on earth." Press button and doors allow way inside United States, accessing target family to harvest.

Only one step with foot, operative me to defile security of degenerate American snake nest. Den of evil. Hive of corruption. Host family of operative me waiting, host arms elbow bent to flutter host fingers in attention of this agent. Host family shouting, arms above with wiggling finger.

For official record, host father present as vast breathing cow, blowing out putrid stink diet heavy with dead slaughterhouse flesh, bellowing stench of Viagra breath during cow father reach to clasp hand of operative me. From tissue compress rate of father fist, bone-to-cow ratio, host father contain 31.2 percent body fat. Wearing is anchored spring apparatus gripping chest blouse pocket of father, one laminated name badge swinging there, giving name "Donald Cedar," from orange dot code, security level nine. Swipe magnetic strip. American industry typical biological exposure indicate strip, as stripe gray along bottom edge of badge, strip showing no recent exposure.

Operative me, am agitating vast fist of cow father, while free hand of this agent reach to acquire security badge.

Next now, host cow father say, "Whoa, there, little fella." Say, "No touchy," and father touching badge, tapping laminate card flat against own cow-stinking chest, say, "Top secret." In talk breath of Viagra, reek of Propecia and mint chew gum.

Operative me ready. Could be simple two pointed elbows to father's chest, one-two, *kam-pow*, Flying Eagle maneuver, and three days, by after next today, will father be vomiting both lungs, turned inside out with massive blood, dead. Fast as easy, young child able do.

Host mother dig pointed elbow into rib cage of host father, say, "Listen to you, Mister Big Shot."

Host mother present as blinking chicken, chin of face bony sharp as beak, chin tucking and swivel to turn, never still, chicken mother say, "Look at you!" Face exploded in silent screaming of wide-open lips and teeth, pointy tongue, eyebrows jumped into chicken forehead. Bony claws of chicken mother, gripping each this agent hands, mother lifts to spread arms too high on top this agent head. Spreading operative me so open, exposed, host mother say, "Look how *skinny*!"

Looped around one bony chicken claw, keys of automobile rattle and swinging. American-type model require 17.1 minute merely so feed gasoline tank full. Keys of host family residence structure. Other automobile keys, crushed between bony chicken claw and hand of operative me. Fingers of this agent close around keys, attempt slip steal begin off from claw.

Next now, host mother say, "We need to put some meat on those bones." Host mother claws keys shut inside mother talon. Sweat sweating from pores of mother, a cooking stew smell heavy mixed with café iced mocha vanilla combined Zoloft mixed Xanax. Stenched with supplement estrogen. Reek of lanolin out face wrinkle with folic acid pills too many.

From tissue flex index of hand, tendon resistance and dermal friction, guessing chicken mother to be 6.3 percent body fat. Blood pressure 182/120. Resting pulse rate 93. Age 42.3 years. Inside six year, easy subject brain stroke dead.

Mother and father, host family name "Cedar." Around operative me, make arms. Grope hug.

Next then, introduced two host sibling.

Host sister push bundle of paper so collide with abdomen of operative me, paper red and constricted with false gold color of synthetic binding tied so make elaborate flowering knot on top. Printed on paper, in English gold letters say, "Happy Birthday."

"It's a T-shirt," say host brother, say, "Show some manners." Host brother only pig dog, cradled on both hands, apparatus of black plastic with pig dog dancing thumbs making buttons beep. Black plastic issue noise many tiny explosion. Machine gun report. Host pig dog brother say, "You're *not* sharing my room, you little turd."

On pig dog breath, the stink of Ritalin. The pollution stench of model airplane adhesive and frequent masturbations. Underneath . . . reek of secret blood, latex rubber, and fear sweat. Pig dog face not look up, but blotted one cheek with vast purple bruised. Estimate old 14.5 years.

Twitching chicken mother, wagging one finger made straight, host mother say, "Now, don't let's be racist . . ."

Easy fast could be, feet of operative me hitting pig dog, *pow-pow*, Flying Giant Stork Death Kick, collapse inside of pig dog zygomatic arch, driving bone back direct to spear brain, *jab-boom*, dead before make next stink breath.

For host mother, soon plan dim mak, fatal touch to acupuncture meridian, leave painless instant now dead as mook Joong dummy.

For official record, only host sister look rewarding opponent. Host sister, stealth cat. Cat of night, silent but eyeing all happen. Cat sister press red paper bundle on fingers of operative me, host sister say, "I hope it fits."

Fingers of operative me cradle package, slick feel of red paper. Pull at fake gold of flowering knot, careful no to tear paper, no to break binding. This agent deconstruct package careful as were delay-ignite Turkish T-155 Panter howitzer shell bomb. Inside, folded black fabric printed white with in letters English writing. Unfold fabric so reveal tunic, wrote across front with "Property of Jesus" on top above shape like fish, like primitive outline caveman fish.

Pig dog eyes looking down at apparatus, twitching thumbs pushing beeps, busy and fast, host brother say, "It's a T-shirt, 'tard." Say, "Put it on."

Fellow mission operatives, neighboring amid arrival for collect luggage, target host families throw arms around, say, "Group hug." Agent Sasha. Agent Vigor. Accept to grip thread of silver floating bladder, English worded "Welcome to Jesus." Other floating bladder worded "Smile!" Other package covered of paper. Other agents buried in heavy layer American arms. Every American try secret to be sniffing operatives, scrub with small snake eyes for soil or foreign disease germ. Host families with fellow operatives trailing more distant, strolling more distant until disappear out airport doors to where already automobile wait. Horn honking at edge of outside street. All automobile the big of house.

Begins here phase one: Operation Havoc.

Arms of operative me wrestle black fabric over head, pull

fabric down over shoulders, over waist until black hang to knees, past knees. Edge of little sleeve hang to elbow. Word of "Jesus" flap over crotch. Collar big around to circle neck and one shoulder of this agent.

Breathing cow father say, "You'll grow into it." Say, stinking fluoride breath, "Here," and hand over fabric rag glued to hang off end of wood stick. American flag little as napkin. White, red, and blue.

Fingers of operative me pinch wood stick like stem of stinking weed. Wave stripe flag to fan away reek of host family air. Butter fat stench. Chemical hair soap stink. Such filthy reek American cash money.

Hand of vast cow father, hand rise, all finger made straight as for pledge. Lips host father say, "We're not *just* a family." Say shout, "We're a *team*!"

Same now, host mother flex both leg limbs so able leap, smite own palm against open hand of father, making loud sound of slap hands. Say shout host chicken mother, *"Team Cedar!"*

Begins here delicious tang of host family, thin American blood already salt on hot tongue of operative me. Already is decadent host family flesh tear by operative teeth. Drool of operative me, flooding hunger within mouth making to swallow. Tongue to lick lips of operative me. Drown cyanide molar. Could be crunch of host bones sweet between teeth of this agent. Stomach to growl. Quick them to be screaming out blood, mouth trumpet yawning blood, quick dead. Ultimate vengeance.

Label tag inside collar of Jesus tunic, print "Made in China."

Label tag along weed stem of American flag, print "Made in China."

Operative me not say loud, only say inside this agent head, quote turncoat Hebrew, corrupt genius Robert Oppenheimer, atom bomb father, quote, "I am become as death, the destroyer of worlds." Next then, making agent eyes bright on host target family, mouth of operative design into smile, extra especial wide to show all of many sharp white teeth.

Quote, "All the better to eat you with, my dears."

Repeat inside head of operative me, quote, "I am become as death . . ."

Chicken mother say, "We'll make an American out of you . . ." Keys of automobile jangling, beak chin wagging no stop, host mother say, "Or, swear to our Lord almighty God, we are gonna die trying."

Dispatch Second

Begins here second account of operative me, agent number 67, on arrival retail product distribution facility of city ▓▓▓▓▓. Outlet number ▓▓▓▓▓. Date ▓▓▓▓▓. For official record, during American winter youth attend compulsive levels of teaching; during summer, American youth must attend shopping mall.

Magic quiet door go sideways, disappear inside wall to open path from outside. Not total all glass, extruded aluminum metal frame silver edge, doors slide gone until reveal inside stand old woman, slave woman appareled with red tunic, spring apparatus gripping tunic front to hang swinging sign, printed, "Doris." Ancient sentinel rest gray cloud eye upon operative me, roll eye from hair and down this agent, say, voice like old parrot, say, "Welcome to Wal-Mart." Say, "May I help you find something?"

Mouths of this agent make smile, face design into pleasing eye contact. This agent say, "Much venerate ancient mother . . . where sold here location China-make 81-S-type gas-operated, rotating-bolt, fire six hundred fifty rounds per minute machine gun?"

Face of ancient mummify bound in dying skin, clouded eye only look, no blink.

Smile of operative me say, "Revered soon dying mother, distribute you ammunitions correct for Croatia-made forty-five-caliber, long-piston-stroke APS assault rifle?"

Smile of operative me, breathing, await.

Sag windpipe of ancient parrot, sag skin jump with swallow. Edge smear of red wax slice open as mouth, wax smile melt flat, straight.

"Brazil-made FA 03 assault rifle?" say this agent, shout, maybe not could hear, shout, "Venerate ancestor, much respected dying soon rotting corpse," shout, "where sell here Slovak SA Vz.58 assault rifle?"

Parrot face of dying skin fill with blood glow, red wax of mouth bunch until volcano pucker, tight until skin of pucker mouth pinched white of no blood. Cloud eyes flash electric bolts. Volcano blow open, old parrot voice say, loud shout, saliva erupt to fly, "You'll find our sporting goods on aisle sixteen, young man."

Could be, *zing-wring*, hands of this operative pounce in rapid Bird Wing Gentle Embrace to twist parrot neck, backbone *twist-snap*, to bring mercy instant soft death.

Merely this agent say, "Thank you, much esteemed madam living skeleton." Wish safe quick soon mission into next eternity.

For official record, squirrel maze of retail distribution center puzzle of competition warring objects, all improved, all package within fire colors. Area divided into walls constructed from objects, all tinted color so grab eye. All object printed: Love me. Look me. Million speaking objects, begging. Crown American consumer with power of king, to rescue choose and give home or abandon here for expire. Word label blow sharp into ear, loud into eye. Pander hand to take. Dying objects. All here, useful life winding down in clock ticks. Dying objects. Dying buyer. Dying slave woman "Doris." Desperate how sad.

Feet of this operative walk bending around corners, through

canyon shadowed of objects, all boast best cheap. All most good taste. All objects fight for adopt.

Bending around new corner, eyes of operative me witness operative Tibor, agent 23, shoving wheeled silver basket of host family. Around new corner, witness operative Magda, agent 36; host mother eyeing sideways as concealing bright box of object within tunic of that agent to theft. Eye of operative Magda meeting eye contact of this agent.

Recent to commence: Operation Havoc.

Next then, feet of this operative bending around new corner, witness host brother, pig dog, resting on polish floor. Prone on floor, pig dog face cheek flat pressed on floor, whole body sprawl behind head and neck. Stand over, other new youth, American growing clear-yellow hair to hang hiding ears. Clear-yellow hair hang to hide neck, hang so curtain sides of face while youth rest shoe foot on upside of pig dog face. Clear-yellow youth balance all weight, stand only on face of host brother, clear-yellow youth say, "Hand over the cash, dick-wad..."

Face of pig dog, pinched under shoe, flat on top of floor, nose of host brother leak blood and liquid mucus in mix puddle around crack lips. Host brother eyes squeeze shut. Lips of pig dog sputter in puddle, blow blood and juice to say, "Okay...okay." Say, "Just let me up."

Clear-yellow bully reach hand to behind trouser pocket of pig dog. Slide fingers within and pull until denim fabric cry with threads breaking, until pocket flap hanging like fabric tail. Hands of clear-yellow bully, stomp shoe planted to hold pig dog face into floor, hands apprehend American paper dollars out of leather pocketbook of pig dog. Clear-yellow bully stuff paper in own trouser pocket, throw hollow pocketbook to wing, *zing-pow*, bounce against face, splashing blood puddle of host brother. Clear-bully look to witness this agent, eyes of bully electric-bolt blue, product fire color blue, to grab eyes of operative me. Bully appareled with black tunic lettered, "John 3:16." Blue denim trouser. Clear-yellow bully say, "What are you looking at, pygmy?" Say, "Beat it!"

Eyes of host brother open, look from floor, lips say, "I told you not to *follow* me ..." Eyes zigzag cracked with blood tunnels inside white part.

Leather pocketbook spread open on floor, splashed in blood, hollow of dollars. Knees of operative me bend so allow hands of this agent to retrieve.

Clear-yellow bully say, "Hey, Cedar, is this your little colored bitch?"

Hold pocketbook slippery wet in blood, this agent say, "No pygmy."

Clear-yellow bully, foot stand on cowering pig dog, yellow hair swing across fire blue eye, bully say, "You a gook? A nigger? A sand flea?" Say, "Exactly what breed of wetback bitch are you?"

Could be, this instant, elbows of operative me fly and drive fast, *wham-pow*, to soft corners of head temple, stun brain of yellow bully. Blackout. Foot of this agent stomp down trouser waist of bully to pool around bully feet. Next then turgid weapon of operative me, violate stunned anus, humiliate with seed the forced screaming pain of clear-yellow bully. All dry friction.

Clear-yellow bully lift shoe from head of host brother. Fashions face of half smile, says, "Okay, Cedar, you can go fuck your little colored bitch." Say, "Thanks for the cash." Shoe of bully step in puddle of blood, and clear-yellow bully print blood in zigzag design of shoe bottom going away, blood design of diagonal traction lines going less red, less clear until feet bend around new product wall corner, gone.

Solely remain trail blood steps.

Solely witness, peek from terminus product aisle Doris woman cadaver squinting for watch melee. Next now, cadaver scuttle, scurry retreat, vanished.

Pig dog lift own self to rest on both elbow against floor. Zigzag engraved, embedded in cheek of host brother face. Dermis patterned dark pink, later red, later purple in shoe traction design. Diagonal many line of purple electric bolts, channels carry water bleed out eyes down, zigzag switchback far as pig dog hand slap water gone.

Finger of operative me, made straight to direct eye, this agent say, "Tennis shoe," at blood design on floor. Next, embed design in cheek.

And pig dog brother slap eye water off own face, say, "No, you stupid pygmy..." Say, "That's a fucking *track shoe*." Zigzag red and white stripe down cheek, like American flag flutter in wind. Host brother scoop air with hand, say, "Follow me."

Next then, pig dog make operative me small parade until where many million shoe for sell area. Shoe on wall shelf. Pile shoe burden many table. Shoe craft from leather like pocketbook remain inside fingers of operative me, glued this agent with colding blood. Shoe craft from fabric like hanging pocket tail of host brother.

Pig dog inhale dripping of nose blood, gurgle, make straight finger at each shoe, say, "That's a tennis shoe, you little pygmy." Make finger at new shoe. "That's a track shoe." Make finger at other new shoe, one after other, say, "Bowling shoe...wrestling shoe...basketball shoe...cross-training shoe...volleyball shoe...baseball shoe...walking shoe...football...soccer..." Only all shoe make finger at, every shoe appearance alike. All shoe twin. No different.

Next then, feet parading around new corner, pig dog discover place many baby animal imprison. Silver cage like wheeled cage shoved by operative Tibor, agent 23, only trap for baby dog, grouping several baby dog. Next new cage, other breed baby dog. Other cage, baby cat. Wall builded cage bricks of baby cat and dog on top and below, all baby animal cry. Stand on silver wire or nest asleep curls of wood. Other wall, cage of baby rodent, many breed rat or mouse. Same as laboratory. Other wall, glass cage of snake and lizard. Heavy in air animal stink, bubble noise out water bin of fire-colored fish.

Pig dog brother make finger straight at wall cages, say, "This, pygmy, is what you'd call a fancy restaurant." Make finger straight at baby dogs and say, "That's called 'beef.'" Say, "Pick one out, and they kill it and dress it right here. I swear." Make straight finger at baby cat and say, "That's pork." Make finger at rat, lizard, snake, baby rabbit, say, "Chicken...veal... fish...crab..."

Head of operative me rock own chin up and down to make agreement.

"Yum-yum," say host brother, smiling bruise zigzag face, hand rubbing circle around own belly. Say, "Them's good eating." Take back hollow pocketbook.

Next then, feet parading around new corner, pig dog discover wall of bottles inside filled gold liquid, clear bottles. Making eyes sideways, both ways fast, host brother twist open top cap of bottle so expose liquid. Pig dog say, "Hold your hands out, pygmy, open side up."

Operative me make hands in front, cupped to ceiling.

Pig dog pour gold liquid too deep inside hands of this

agent. Gold liquid flooding to splash on floor. Host brother twist cap lid closed over bottle, replace on shelf. Say, "Go ahead, pygmy." Slap both of own hands, flat open on own bruise face smudging blood there. Say, "Like that." Say, "It's called 'aftershave.'"

Open hands of operative me splash gold liquid on cheeks of this agent. Mimic to rub liquid around face and neck. Gold sting, smell hot poison, reek to make eyes bleed water, medicine stench scald burn skin of operative me.

"Aftershave," repeat say pig dog brother, say, "Drives the fine ladies wild."

Printed in English letter, word letter black against white label of bottle, English letter spell, "Listerine."

This agent, eye of operative me suffering fire pain, say how in America told all ladies glad liberated to always expose many fragrant vaginas. No ever possess maidenhead. Develop hobby of enjoying many frequent abortion. Always hungering to fashion moist lady mouths tight around gentlemen genital.

Pig dog brother merely rest eye on this agent. Eye no blink.

Mouth of operative me say, "Is no correct?"

Host pig dog say, "I wish..." Swinging smudge blood face from side then side, say, "Little pygmy, from your mouth to God's ear."

Inside head of operative me fashion image of host sister. Sister, cat eyeing all happen. Stealth cat image inflate turgid weapon within trouser of this agent.

Next then, feet parading around new corner, pig dog discover door printed English letter word *Men*. Displayed there outline picture man, two arm, two leg.

Pig dog say, "This here's called a spa." Make finger straight at door, say, "You go in here, and they got bowls of water set on the floor. The cleanest, freshest water in these United States." Say, "You only have to kneel down and you can drink all you want." Pig dog eyes no blink. Mouth no smile. Say, "Go try it. You'll love the taste." Host brother hand push "Men" door open to reveal inside walls white tile, floor tile.

Only one step with foot, operative me cloaked within smell, reek like baby animal restaurant. Stench of too many sulfur-base amino acid. Diet heavy with dead flesh. Cola soda of sodium benzoate combine citric acid inside intestine to mix benzene until trigger cancer. Reek of cancer bowel. Fecal impacted colon stink.

Nose of operative me solitary within spa room, door swing close behind this agent.

Several bowl of glazed ceramic hang in row from wall. Metal wall screen several small booth holding water drinking bowl on floor inside each. Rolls paper napkins ready hang from metal wall beside each water bowl, for to wipe mouth. Exact as pig dog teach.

Next then, door of one small booth swing open fast to, *swish-bang*, collide white tile wall behind. Metal door boom open and voice say, "Hey, pygmy..." Male voice say, "Yo, little bitch..."

Clear-yellow hair hanging. Electric-bolt blue eye. Black tunic lettered, "John 3:16." Blue denim trouser holding pocket of thefted paper money. Clear-yellow bully jerk head, swing eyes from behind yellow hair curtain. Bully say, "You come from one of those dick-mutilation places?" Say, "Whip it out, pygmy." Say, "Show me what the witch doctor done to you..."

Flash fire quick instant. *Wham-crack*. Bone elbows spear-pointed sharp bent to soar, Soaring Eagle Double Strike to left-right temple soft spots of bully forehead. Hard hit, *zing-crunch*, to hammer through layer of yellow hair. Clear-yellow bully to stun, crumple, knees bent, torso collapse topple to white tile floor.

Hand of operative me grip back waistband of trouser, luggage bully into metal booth, by waistband handle throw bully face against tile wall to straddle water drinking bowl. Bully blackout asleep. Skeleton bones loose. Head moaning. Knee of operative me bend to plant impact on lower backbone of bully to force back arch, protrude bully anus. Knee bend to stomp foot of this agent down, *rip-pow*, toe inside back waistband and drop trousers to wrinkle fabric pool around bully ankles. Foot of operative me stamp down inside shorts of clear-yellow bully.

Face sideways flat clobber into tile wall, bully blue eye flutter, eye cover skins flicker, blink, flicker, come open. Bully mouth biting sideways into tile say, "What the fuck?"

One hand operative me open down own trouser zipper. One hand operative me fingers fold into pointed snake head, dart strike, *zip-bam*, Mighty Python Smother, to cram into bully mouth, pushing until knuckles of operative me force teeth too wide apart, no bite able, until fingers cork bully windpipe face skin so tint pink, red, more-dark red.

Hands of bully scramble claw to remove mouth Python Smother. Bully face full tinting to electric-bolt blue of eye. Face skin blue, eye cover skin flutter, all muscle go tense to starting loose. Starving air, relax. Exposed anus of bully, same smooth of ceramic tile, tinting from pink to blue. Nested in cleavage of pale buttock, blue pucker only remain pinch hard from self-defend.

Weapon of operative me sprouted, ready. Turgid. Exposed out zipper. Dripping ready. One hand of operative me cork bully windpipe. One hand pin-cupped back of bully neck so plant face against wall tile, bully blood leak out nose, sliding red stripe from nose down white tile wall. American flag, red and white stripes sliding to tile floor. Blue face, nose folded sideways. Seeing stars. Neck hand of operative me make finger straight to dig nail, sharp shovel into pucker pinch blue anus muscle.

All body of bully suffocated, only still seizure every muscle as straight fingernail drill through pucker and pull sideways to stretch open hole. Pry. Force open, dry, all friction, all peel of tender membrane until dripping head of weapon wedge room in twist of muscle.

One stroke. Hips of operative me shove full deep, belly deep, ram until bully stand only on foot toes try to escape.

Bully mouth scream hot saliva around embedded hand of this agent. Screams trapped, shaking so vibrate whole body inside corked hand of operative me. Fingers cupped, fist grabbed full of scream and blue tongue. Curtain yellow hair drip sweat.

Weapon of this agent, stabbing, hollowing blue hole, scraping friction until full drive deep inside whole long of self. Next then retreating to pop free, dripping. Next again, stab full deep. All time, mouth of operative me flogging with English word *bitch*. Flogging close into cold blue ear, into curtain of clear-yellow hair swinging, flogging, "Bitch" and "Bitch" and "Bitch."

Electric-bolt eyes of bully bleeding water. Blue star of fighting anus leak blood into thin stripes down white legs. Everywhere patriotic. Here so great American nation.

Dry drag weapon out blistered blue hole. Paint white stripe seed of operative me, spray-painting thick clots sliding down bully legs. One hand of operative me seize back of black tunic fabric, printed "John 3:16," to clean weapon of blood, wipe stink of brown fecal, white smear of seed. Abandon tunic mixed mess of stench stained. Abandon own seed. Abandon clear-yellow bully, leg spread, mouth gape to gasp air, anus inside peeled out so protrude. Leaking nasty drip.

Final last gesture, fingers of this agent fish leather pocketbook from out behind pocket of bully trouser. Obtain out entire paper money bills. No only pig dog money, all money, numbers and numbers of money. Drop hollow pocketbook between striped bully legs, splash, into water drinking bowl.

Gasping voice of bully sob, gargle mucus and saliva, croak so say, "I'm gonna fucking kill you, pygmy." Sob, cough, sniff and sob. Bully cough blood against tile wall to say, "You hear me, pygmy, you're already a dead wetback..."

Mouth of operative me say, quote politic father Karl Marx, quote, "'History repeats itself, first as tragedy, second as farce.'" This agent wash clean own hands. Exit spa to where pig dog, one foot tapping on floor, arms making folded so cross chest, host brother say, "Geez, pygmy...did you fall in?" Remain on face purple electric-bolt stomp pattern. Fabric tail hang between legs.

Quote, "History repeats itself, first as tragedy, second as farce."

Ready hand of operative me reach to give, hand across thick layer of paper bills smear stained blood, fecal, seed, sweat, stinking saliva, a fortune typical American cash money.

Dispatch Third

Begins here third account of operative me, agent number 67, on arrival religion propaganda distribution outlet of city ██████. Outpost community ████████. Date ████████. For official record, if become bankrupt old retail distribution centers—labeled supermega, so-enlarged foodstuff market— later reincarnate to become worship shrine. First sell foodstuff, next then same structure sell battered furnitures, next now born as gymnasium club, next broker flea markets, only at final end of life...sell religions.

Example here, pig dog brother inform, location where former time heads multiple cabbage mounted to build pyramid pile for marketing display, current now location occupy with fake statue plaster dead male, fake torture dead on two crossed stick, fake blood painted red hand and foot. Worship shrine offer haircut parlor, franchise designer ice creams, Internet computers lab. Feature vast black macadam sea of parking automobile.

Location former chew gum, chocolate snack, salted chips of potato, current now occupy with cylinder white paraffin encase burning string, many tiny single fire. Location former bright-color breakfast objects boasting most taste, most little price, recent best vitamins, current now feature bunches severed genitals of rose plants, vagina and penis of daisy and carnation plants, flaunted color and scent of many inviting plant life sex organs.

Location former alcohol products provided behind refrigerator glass, only distribute with aged identification, current now instrument of keyboard sounding random notes generated gas forced through bellows, control using hand and foot of venerate living skeleton. Same esteemed madam soon rotting corpse encounter at magic door Wal-Mart.

Host vast breathing cow father, make small parade to where living corpse seated to control noise keyboard. Host father say, "Mrs. Lilly?" Say, "I'd like to introduce our new foster son." Say, "We call him 'Pygmy.'"

As custom, feet of operative me step to nearby. Hand extend to accept hand of acclaimed wrinkle cadaver. Mouth wish pleasant passing to become again useful soil.

Most respected dying rot mummy rest clouded eye upon this agent. Split red wax of face lips so reveal white prosthetic teeth nested behind, say, "We've already met..."

Next now, this agent charged by advancing male, brandishing with open hand, fingers engaging those of operative me. Man, viper, crushing fingers as coiled around goat for kill and swallow. Shaking arm as dog breaks backbone of rat. Predator male, slaughter arm of this agent, say, "Pleased to meet you, Pygmy." Say, "I'm Reverend Tony."

Mouths of operative me say, "Happy to engage you, crafty stooge of superstition."

Mouths of operative me say, "How is your health, puppet of Satan?"

Worship leader fashion forehead to lift single hair brow arching above eye. Devil Tony preserve smile. Say, "This little young 'un needs to practice his English."

Hand of operative me begin compact fingers of worship leader, to grind, bones collapse, skin muscle press so wring of moisture, squeeze as fabric rag soaked in blood. Could be, with pointed knee, *sock-block*, explode worship leader rib cage.

Could be, crash head into reverend head, *butt-bang*, contusion brain. Instead, merely this agent say, "Meet repeat soon, please, licking viper of evil."

Worship leader snatch retreat crushed hand, cradle in other own hand. Crushed hand wrung white, leader say, "If you'll excuse me, we have a new lamb to welcome into our flock this morning." Cast eye upon this agent, devil Tony say, "If I'm not mistaken, little Pygmy, our new lamb comes from your own colorful native land..."

Here worship shrine, all male neck must bind around with knotted banner, silk banner knotted at windpipe so dangle two long strands down chest to waistband trouser. All female must shelter head inside hat cover. Location enter accompany breathing cow father, twitching chicken host mother, pig dog brother, and host cat sister. Make small parade until seated long bench.

Strategic station, positioned among venomous Christian vipers, seated operative Ling, agent 19; operative Tibor, agent 23; operative Bokara, agent 54; operative Sheena, agent 7. Eyes of all operative, witness, monitor, scrub worship location. Hone sharp fangs. Prepare: Operation Havoc.

In distant, behind swinging curtain of clear-yellow hair, purple bruise surrounding both eye, nose folded to sleep sideways against one bruise face cheek—clear-yellow bully electric-bolt blue eye rest on operative me. All muscle stiff from hate. Bully mouths parted one end reveal teeth clench behind. Single front tooth, corner chip.

Remain embed on bully face cheek square grid lines of ceramic tile grout.

Stealth cat, host sister say, "Poor Trevor." Sister cast eye on clear-yellow bully, say, "He looks like he was in a car wreck..." During host sister rest eye long away to clear-yellow bully, sister vent all gas out lung, single long breathing, shoulder melt, host sister head wilt to one side, hang slanted, cat mouth make smile, say, "Trevor Stonefield is so dreamy..." Sister hand lift to touch location own heart muscle.

Clear-yellow bully fire blue eye no blink. Muscle spasm clench both corner bully jaw. Blood tunnels descend from jaw, worming thick under skin, swelled, many branch to vanish behind fence of white blouse collar bound around bully neck with knotted silk banner, narrow banner stripe red then blue. Face of clear-yellow bully fill with blood glow. Mouth edges together pinched white of no blood. Arm hang, no bend, only beneath wrist collars of blouse sleeve fingers fisted, also stony white of no blood.

Head cover of cat sister, embellish with fake petunia genital craft of fabric. Red color, yellow color. Crowning hair, suggest many ready vaginas. Eye of host sister remaining rest upon clear-yellow bully, remain smile, cat sister say, "I wonder what Trevor's like in bed..."

Both shoulder of operative me spasm to rise near ear, make shrugged, say, "Bitch anus rough scabbed too narrow around in scar tissue."

Immediate, cat sister eye rest upon this agent. Sister eye go round, skin of face smooth open, mouth hang until say, "For your information, he's *straight*."

For official record, dermis of cat sister indicate harboring full many viable human egg for reproduction of future operative. Within cotton bodice, mammary swell to manufacture diet for many future agent. Judging long strand hair, no break, no dry, no louse, cat sister vector no disease. Pelvis function easily to accept seed, then alternate issue constant offspring. Loins needing much seed.

Weapon of operative me moving turgid within trouser of

this agent. Scrotum constrict size. Must saliva of operative me swallow.

Eye elsewhere location, cat sister say, "Who's the *skank?*"

This agent follow sister eye through religion peoples, beyond clear-yellow bully and fragrant severed genitals of variety plants life. Ignited threads embedded within cylinder white paraffin, to below crossed wood sticks where hang naked fake male painted fake blood on hands, feet.

Cat sister eye rest below fake torture male.

Eye of this operative discover that location, standing, mouth tight as fist, eyeing back, operative Magda, agent 36. Electric bolt out Magda brown eye, to attack cat sister.

Cat sister say, "You want to talk bitches..." Say, "That one looks like she could kill me."

In Magda hands already knotted finger ready Cobra One-Strike No-Blood, *bam-slam*, inflict cat sister instant dead. More fast most eye able look.

For official record, operative Magda sole state designate reproductive coagent operative me. Forever permanent. Extensive chromosome test establish best premium coagent, assigned from birth, only Magda egg to fertilize. Agent 36 egg apportioned legal property solely operative me copulate. Atop vagina of that operative, noble best duty must lifetime fornicate.

For official record, during current now, eye of operative me rest on operative Magda. Magda brown eye rest on host cat sister. Sister eye rest on bruised clear-yellow bitch, Trevor Stonefield. Bully eye rest on this agent. Eye of four persons describe rough square within worship shrine.

Voice say, break into head of operative me, male voice say, "My, my..."

Voice worship leader eye cat sister and this agent, devil

Tony say, "I do believe that love has found Andy Hardy." Fashion face of half smile. Blink eye at operative me.

Next then shrine filled roaring noise. Bellows powering keyboard instrument tremble atmosphere, fill with location wind noise. Baying out mouths all worship member, wailing, scream word off insides paper book unfolded in hand. Baying cacophony of gaping fish mouth, all gape unison, head tilted backward to rest eye against fake torture male painted blood. Many dog bay at moon. Shrine air fogged many stink breath. Barking. During herd dog bay, all eye on fake moon, fake blood, fake metal spike, fake protrude fake male feet.

Eye of operative me look up, look under loincloth where only plaster. No weapon. Plaster no painted. Layer on fake feet blood, old dust. Painted blood out plaster hat cover of sharp sticks, plaster eye bleed water painted blue.

Under foot of fake male, bin filled water, big of swim bath. Located there operative Magda appareled gown sewn white fabric. Belted around waist. Feet revealed below gown naked, belted around neck gold chain of metal suspending miniature of fake torture man burdening crossed stick. Cold shark eye of operative Magda rest on this agent. Behind heels of naked feet yawn water bin. Filled deep of clear water. Located front, elevated. Worship leader stance agent 36 to edge of bin, backside to deep water.

Worship leader cup both hand in air, patting air until baying stop. Bellowing keyboard stop. "Dear brothers and sisters," say devil Tony, "we've come together on this beautiful Sunday to welcome a shining new lamb into the bosom of Christ."

Among the worship, Magda look at cat sister look at clear-yellow bully look at operative me.

Worship leader during say, "As John the Baptist washed clean the sins of Christ, let us also redeem the soul of this pagan child." During say, devil Tony step out of own shoe. Step foot over lip of bin, immersing own trouser in water. Immersing more deep until water deep lap to own trouser waistband. Leader finger open button own blouse, tuck neck banner inserted between gap placket blouse, weave button fastener returned through hole. Silk banner safe so no fish into water.

Face muscle of operative Magda spasm, smooth becoming mountains, canyons, as worship leader hands grab from behind, pull backward to topple agent 36 backward toward water. Could be *bam-chop*, could be jump, Magda tuck legs, Leaping Kangaroo Punch Escape, pulverize sternum of worship man, leap free of water bin and retreat. Could be, except no. Agent 36 permit hands carry backward down until buried in water. Eyes of agent look up through lens of shifting clear water, look during mouth of worship man move.

Waters swallow operative Magda. Agent 36, official womb of future operative.

Hands spread to remain agent submerge, worship leader say, "Let us pray..."

Lungs of operative Magda suffer air starvation.

Mouth of worship leader say, "We wash clean this child, born into the bogus faith of a false prophet. The misguided lies of a dead Mohammad or Buddha or Hindi." Say, "In this immersing, let this child die and be reborn in the name of the one true everlasting Lord." Say, "Let this death be not in vain, but may this tiny child arise in perfect union with Jesus Christ..."

From embedded water, read lips of worship leader, ears of operative Magda decipher only, "Dead...die...death..."

Is making of agent 36 human sacrifice. Both lung of that agent crave hanker for oxygen.

Fellow Christian viper serving all seated upon benches, serving plates heaped many monetary notes. Stinking feast many cash denominations. Plates filled mass legal tender. Seated vipers feeding plates, paper money dollar out pocketbook. Host chicken mother, bony claw gut innards of shoulder purse until retract crumple cash money, feed to hungry plate. Abandon plate to host father. Cow father abandon hungry plate to cat sister.

Just as rapid, stealth operative Tibor abscond paper fortune from plate. Operative Chernok secret purloin much lucre.

Hand of worship leader shove retain sternum Magda embedded water. Opposite hand of leader flat palm held above own head full-length straight arm, open to inside of roof. Arm made straight at roof, both eye close. Mouthing lip of devil Tony say, "May this tiny child of God perish and be reborn in perfection."

Torso of worship leader tilted over water surface of bin. Legs of leader rooted in water neighboring operative Magda. Leader mouth move, say, "We ask only that this humble child open her heart to the goodness of Your blood . . ."

Next then, silk striped banner of worship leader, out tuck from between placket at front of leader blouse. From tuck between buttons, banner flutter, dangle, flop so settle in water liquid, sink snaking spiral into clear water to tickle, lack of air, face of operative Magda. Both hand of that agent erupt out flat water, snatch tight fist around striped banner. Dual arms pull until, *flash-splash*, topple, embed devil Tony full in liquid. Famish for oxygen.

Inside head of operative me echoing English word *blood*. Echoing *dead*. Echoing *sacrifice*.

Magda pull wrestle worship leader buried in water, agent

36 seize full wrapped arm and leg. Force leader helpless. Captured, thirsting to inhale.

For official record, nest American Christian vipers no able venture into water bin. Only witness, so fast occur. Vipers seated steps below bin level, below fake blood statue, below burning paraffin and bunched genital of plant life. View from vipers, witness leader man sunk into water. Gone. Next then, water splash froth, wash out edge of bin. Next then, water smooth still flat. No bubble. No viper move, only await.

Operative Bokara extract of hungry plate rich sum cash money. Operative Oleg deduct stinking fortune capitalist nation dollars.

Could be, embed deep, ruthless hand of Magda, *pop-pop*, make drilling Barracuda Deadly Eye Gouge. Could be teeth, *zip-chomp*, Piranha Strike, major blood tunnel at windpipe savage chew.

Mouth lips of operative me quote glorious tyrant Mao Tse-tung, total to admire, quote, "Women hold up half the sky."

Next then, red cloud bloom in water, red billowing in water, more dark red until no clear. Until generate all Christian viper rush to bin edge, no more able witness into water. Opaque red. No wave or bubble or splash. Only devil Tony and agent 36 gone, buried, full below red liquid.

Settled full deep against floor of water bin, Magda fisting neck banner of worship leader, hands of that agent grip tight to starve oxygen. Allow leader once time heave up, leaping dolphin, break surface of red liquid, leader eye bulge, mouth devour air. Hands of leader climbing air ladder. White blouse, hair flat down sides face, streaking blood, red.

Next now, arms of operative Magda streaked blood jerk leader back to floor of bin.

Worship man scream bubble burst from water. Next now, silent.

Allow red surface smooth, no bubble. All Christian viper twist together own hands, breathing seized. Surface flat of water bin, full smooth, full red. No more leader splash up.

No worship leader able visible. No visible Magda.

Christian plate hungry for money, arrive, cat sister abandon plate to pig dog.

"Geez, Pygmy," say pig dog host brother, remain sit, squinting peer over edge of bin. Pig dog hand pinching paper American dollar out own trouser. Host brother say, "Just when you thought it was safe to go back in the baptism font..." Host brother hand release cash dollar into money plate, paper bill smear stained fingerprints of blood, reek of Trevor bitch anus, seed of operative me.

Next then, cat host sister say, "Gross!" Say, "What is that smell?" Wave hand so clear away air surrounding own nose, blink eye cover skins and fashion squint eye upon operative me.

Quote, "Women hold up half the sky."

Host sister say, "Pygmy, did you take a bath in *Listerine*?"

Dispatch
Fourth

Begins here fourth account of operative me, agent number 67, seated among sleeping vault of host sister. Domestic structure Cedar. Suburb community ██████. Date ██████. For official record, have no yet violated secure entry host sister vagina. More easy this agent able violate secure American nation border.

Current now, curving sinew spiraling tail of smoke arise white out tip solder iron, smoke drawing pattern in air, iron perched between cat finger like cigarette holder old film, host sister brandish, say, "Hey, Pygmy, when school starts..." Say, "Are you going out for science fair?"

Mouths of operative me say, "Define?"

Cat sister squint eye at heat, molten solder liquid lead metal atop work surface, say, "It's easy." Making solder electric circuits, say, "You invent something bullshit and they give you a free trip to the city." Bunch shoulders at own ears, make shrugged, say, "But science is totally the hot where-it's-at."

Ear of operative me steady consume sister word, only no able decipher. This agent sit balanced upon edge host sister bed, mattress pile with blanket, patterned many animals of brown weave through cover blanket. Animal all smile. Brown animal clench string bound to floating bladder inflated helium. Silly animal.

Host sister drip and draw in melted lead metal, breathing snake tail of smoke.

Host sister bed vault, all plaster surface colored yellow

paint. Floor, layered yellow matting crafted with million strands yarn. Window observe leaves of outside tree. Light craning on stork neck illuminate where sister sit, tilt to watch where solder melt. Electric bulb of light strong bright.

Door position, healed. Next now, rap, rap, rap knocking opposite surface of door. Other room voice say, "Sweetheart, can I borrow some batteries?"

Host sister, cat sister remain head tilted. Eye rest on tip solder wand. Say, "What size?"

Door swing so reveal host chicken mother, claw gripping opposite handle. Mother say, "Knock, knock." Eyes rest upon operative me, smile same fake as brown animal patterned in blanket. Chicken mouth say, "Double-A, triple-A, I'll take whatever you got."

No look away solder project, cat sister say, "Try my radio." Say, "They're D-sized, but they're pretty new."

Chicken mother strut small parade to table, side of bed. Claw scratch open hatch in behind black plastic box contraption. Spill from, one to eight cylinders, land *plop-plop* on bedcover blanket. Cylinder bounce and roll. Host mother gather, bony talon hand secure eight into trouser side pockets. Mouth say, "Any more?"

Veiled within smoke, haloed and misted pale smoke of hot metal, sister face say, "Try my Talking Teddy bear."

Mother claws pry open skin of stuffed bear. Miniature false bear. Skin of behind swing open so reveal cylinder, chicken claw scrape hollow. Bear gutted. Conceal battery cylinder into trouser. Mouth say, pitch more high, "Any more?"

Wreathed of metal cigarette holder, glowing hot wand, sister face say nothing. Silent. Nose vent metal smoke. Acrid. Mouth say, "Try my rape siren, in my backpack." Fuming solder smoke, say, "God, Mom, you're pathetic."

Chicken mother strut to location fabric container rest at floor below window. Claw scratch from pocket small trumpet, twist end and void two cylinder. Trouser pocket swollen many cylinders, host mother scramble until door, say, "Thanks, sweetheart." Say, "You two play nice." Drag door until healed into wall. Foot sounds, smaller, gone.

Face tilted, eye cover skin make squint within floating path, curve corkscrew white threads smoke, host sister say, "I can't believe my own mother would put her orgasm above me maybe getting raped..."

Hands shoving metal worm solder metal to melt against heat solder iron. Paint liquid metal pattern on circuit board work project. In breathe snaking white smoke, cat sister say, "Trust me, Pygmy, don't go down to the basement for a while." Say, "Mom's throwing one of her fukkerware parties." Say, "It used to be her and her friends would force each other to buy these plastic boxes for leftover food. Now they sit around test-driving vibrators."

Eyes of operative me solely rest on sister. Beyond sheet window glass, under beyond tree, along sidewalk stand operative Magda, no suffocated, brown eyes rested on here.

Host sister say, "It's these sex toys they use to climax." Say, "That's why the batteries."

Miniature invisible shake grow out bed, spring of mattress, floor of chamber shimmy. Tiny shake make dance yellow fabric window veil. Miniature shimmy shiver innards of operative me, tiny pulse massage weapon within trouser.

Tool knife shiver route across work surface, past host sister elbow, closer edge to drop. Next now, cat sister seize knife one now before drop to floor. Rest knife more far from edge work surface, say, "What torques me is how my mom's generation started a revolution for equal rights and just ended up in the basement jacking off." Say, "But I guess I could make the same complaint about my dad's generation and the Internet..."

Beyond window glass, Magda steady as tree. Rooted. Waited.

Say, stealth calm as green tree sloth, say, "Esteemed host sister, what is labor position of respected father?"

Repeat shoulders made shrugging, cat sister say, "Something with the government. Developing new strains of some virus or something." Eat smoke in mouth, vent burnt metal smoke out nostril.

Speech of operative me, this agent fashion worry scared, say, "Glorious father craft deadly virus?"

Craning light on work surface, throw bright bulb illuminate solder work, next now less bright. Bulb shrink from white to yellow. Dim in room layer white smoke. Next now, repeat glow bright.

Host sister eye bulb, say, "Gross, they've graduated from direct current to alternating."

This agent, say, "Clarify?"

"From battery sex toys to ones that plug into outlets," say host sister. Solder draw into pattern, link diode, transistor, transducer, mystery project, host sister say, "Build a better *vibrator*, Pygmy, and the world will beat a path to your door."

Eye blink against white smoke, cat sister say, "What scares me is how the Chinese are light-years ahead of us in the sex toy race..."

Eye of operative me cast to rest against Magda, outside, ready wait vessel for seed of this agent. Mouths of this agent quote fascist tyrant, lunatic emperor Adolf Hitler, say, "'The day of individual happiness has passed.'"

Host sister say, "What are your folks like?" Sister hair

gather behind head, braided single rope. Sister buttocks cupped in work chair, cat sister say, "I mean, what was your childhood like?" Say, "What's it like where you come from?"

Next then, hands of operative me grip yellow fabric veil window, layer fabrics so meet in center, blocking view tree, outside, Magda. Eclipse.

Quote, "The day of individual happiness has passed."

Next now crane light shining work surface, bulb die black. Smoke no rise white out solder iron. Solder grow cool until weld, stuck to iron. Cat sister say, "Shit." Project hesitated. Say, "Those horny housewives..."

Chamber dim, darken, operative me say, "Clarify?"

Twins of operative me and cat sister seated inside dark, host sister say, "My guess is they've tripped a circuit breaker."

And this agent say, "Revision." Say, "Please, tell repeat nature host father security, government priority top-secret labors?" Say, "Provide more detail, please."

Dispatch
Fifth

Begins here fifth account of operative me, agent number 67 recall training session day ████████. Operative preparation laboratory ████████. Home nation ████████. Dated back many year. For official record, recounting here formative history of operative me.

Depict here standard classroom laboratory occupy basement owning no window. Location divided long aisle between lengthy work surface, wall lined silver bins wove wire housing resident animals. White rodent. Frequent rabbit suffering experiment. Pigs of Guinea. Fellow operatives conduct to test chemical exposing animals. Location reek as baby animal fancy restaurant American shopping mall.

Baby puppy, as American title *beef*. Baby kitten as *pork*.

For official record, as rule must address chemist instructor, during enter room, unison all operative must announce: "Greetings, esteemed most revered educator." In single unite voice must all operative say, "Accept, please, our gratitude for the wisdom you impart." This, every today.

Specific past today, many today ago, this agent heat tincture of iodine, hovering tincture within glass beaker above flame gas burner. One hand of operative me operate beaker secure grasping tongs. One hand of this agent suspend metal saucer filled ice on top boil tincture heated within beaker, crystal iodine sublime as alcohol evaporate. Crystal form, crusted underneath side of ice saucer. Hands of operative me securing heated beaker, gas flame hiss, hand secure to suspend saucer of ice, this agent handless as laboratory go dark. Sudden, no light. From bright, many surrounded fellow operative, Tibor, Sheena, Ling, Metro, Tanek, baby animal, laboratory classroom fall blind dark.

From behind operative me wrap hands of other, cupped to cover eyes of this agent. Cupped dark.

Could be foot heel of operative me backward kick, Exploding Mule, *kick-sock*, to backward shatter knee of attacker. Instead, female voice say, "Comrade operative, fast profess recipe to manufacture vast explosion picric acid." Voice of operative 36, agent Magda.

Duo hands of operative me occupied, one heated, one ice chilled, mouths of this agent say, "Recipe picric acid..." Say, "Twenty aspirin tablet, half cup pure alcohol, sulfuric acid stolen automobile battery, three teaspoon potassium nitrate..."

Cupped hands reek of zinc chloride.

Cupped hands of operative Magda release eyes of this agent. Agent 36 make small parade to stand at elbow of this agent. Magda say, "Exact correct, comrade."

Alcohol of tincture close gone, remaining abandoned iodine crystals frosted underside of metal saucer. Soon, this agent to scrape and collect. Combine most carefully along household cleaner ammonia, generate form nitrogen tri-iodide. Will precipitate red-brown crystals. Wash crystals with alcohol. Wash repeat with ether. Producing next then among most vast explosions learned to humanity.

Peering brown eye to face of operative me, Magda say, "Important must freeze still, comrade." Say, "No motion." Agent 36 poke own fingertip against own face cheek, say, "This location of comrade face, dusted spot white crystals mercury fulminate..."

Very dangerous, caustic, blast when too heated, blast from

any shock. Mercury fulminate. Most old, most no stable explode compound.

Operative Magda raise to point on only foot toes, ballerina poised, to lean near. Breathing of agent 36 brush cheek of operative me. Magda face imminent to contact face skin of this agent. Next then, tongue of operative Magda unfurl out mouth, tongue slippery pink, wet glow, tongue muscle wipe damp path across cheek of this agent.

Cleanse future exploding mercury fulminate.

Next now, hand of operative Magda cup near own mouth, ladylike, screen action as agent 36 salivates protective wad to encase dangerous compound. Next now, Magda expectorate wad salivate against laboratory floor, fast expelled, *zip-slam* into floor where spit compound impact, *flash-boom*, blast leaving crater on concrete.

All fellow operative eyeing. Pigs of Guinea squeal. Sand of concrete raining all agent, stink of smoke, Magda say, "Permit relax, comrade secure now." Repeat expectorate, second salivate produce no blast.

Exhaled breath of Magda stinking sodium hydroxide. Stenched of lead acetate. Could be lips of acetic acid to create deadly chemical reaction, burst when contact sodium bicarbonate lips of this agent.

Next now, unison voice all operative, speaking single voice, say, "Greetings, esteemed most revered educator."

Door of classroom laboratory no longer healed in wall. Door swing so display respected chemist instructor, acclaimed mentor, brilliant leader. Unite wave of voice, all operative say, "Accept, please, our gratitude for the wisdom you impart."

Instructor bow head.

Operative all bow head.

Acclaimed leader make small parade to wire bin occupied

white rodent. Hand of leader swing hatch door to access, pinch behind skin of rodent neck and remove out wire bin. Hand suspend wiggling rodent shoulder-high during face of instructor rotate to ensure all operative eyeing. Make small parade to edge of empty water bin sunk, flush, into laboratory work surface. In center floor of bin, drain hole. Perched top edge of water bin, spigot flanked metal switches to make gush hot or chilled water.

Operative all eyeballing. Magda, Ling, Tanek, Chernok, all.

Revered instructor place white rodent on floor of empty water bin, near drain hole. Instructor say, "Inside head, make following picture..." Say, "Having returned to house, find wild rodent fallen, trapped within house water bin."

Instructor brandish hand direction rodent, during pink claws scramble over steel metal insides of water bin. Rodent climbing little way, then now sliding to trapped on floor of bin. Rodent pink nose twitching air. Pink eye peering up, out water bin.

Much-brilliant instructor say, "Little dirty animal trapped long duration..." Say, "Much hungry, much thirst, much exhausted..." Instructor rest eye against each operative, Metro and Tibor and Mang, say, "Little animal curl tail tight to protect self. Shake. Shiver filled such terror..."

In water bin, white rodent shiver. Cower. Single drop yellow urine roll stripe from animal to drain hole. Ear of rodent fold flat against back of head. Squeezing self most small as able.

Instructor dangle own hand into bin, so fingers stroke white fur down back of rodent. Stroking fur, say, "Little animal merely desire to survive." Say, "Except animal vector disease." Say, stroking fur, "Little animal dirty, plus instinct plan reproduce..."

Esteemed instructor fashion mouth to display frown. Rotate face to one side, then other side, repeat to make head meaning "no."

Acclaimed instructor say, every today must human follow example given from deity. Action of mercy, say instructor, an insult to eye of deity. Say deity no display such mercy. Say operative acting mercy place self on top, standing on top head of deity. Envision self possess more wisdom deity.

Esteemed instructor say top deity ordains all living creation suffer—wasted disease or screaming wearing covered blood—then must some today all to die. Only tragedy if suffer and die during innocent. No sin, no crime, then extinction not earned. Such waste an affront to deity.

"Because all suffer then die," say instructor, stroking white fur rodent, "then operatives must earn own some today extinction."

Justify future cruelty acts of deity. Make of deity no sadism, instead vast wisdom judge.

Top deity model only correct behavior. Say great wisdom instructor, "All must do unto fellow being what the deity does to all."

If operative frequent kick dog...if strike with slap hand reproductive partner...if operative murder stab fellow, that mimic correct lesson of deity. At some today instant of extinction—could be heart explode or consume toxic foodstuff—that extinction no tragedy, no large waste to offend deity. In truth, extinction sinner great vast pleasure unto deity. More sin, more crime, say instructor, more deity will rejoice upon extinction of operative.

Hand of instructor twist water switch, forcing spigot gush water into bin. First, chilled water. Next then gush begin vent steam, water heating, high heat turning steel floor of bin to dark with temperature. Rodent sliding to escape temperature water, heated floor. Hand twist water switch until more gush, flood more floor. Rodent scramble to climb polish walls of bin, slide back to scald, squealing. Rodent climb and slide. Slide and squeal.

Hand of revered leader dangle to electric switch mounted underneath of work surface. Finger activate electric switch and roar sound erupt from drain hole. Out of hole, shaking din, grinding metal of teeth. Hungry dark hole.

White rodent tumble down steel walls, slide, escape grinding drain, rodent feet scorched red running too fast able eye to witness.

Glorious instructor lift own hand, open palm to face all operative. Hand of oath or pledge. Celebrated instructor say, "Vote." Say, "Current now, with hand, vote: Must we extinguish diseased parasite?"

Hands of operative Ling and Chernok rise to say yes. Hands of Tibor and Mang.

Hand of operative me remain low. Breath trapped lungs. Heart muscle scramble as rodent, battle indoors rib cage. Nose sniff, hard snort, so eye this agent no bleed water. Say inside head, say: *Permit rodent survive.* Say, *Please.*

Hand of operative Magda rise to vote yes. All operative eyeing this agent.

Revered instructor quote total vile tyrant, brutal king Adolf Hitler, quote, "'I do not see why man should not be just as cruel as nature.'"

Hand of this operative rise. Total "yes" in unison. To make single voice.

Today, talented instructor say, this crime is how the West would title as "baptism." Today crime craft operatives present here, a pleasure unto the deity. Dirty sinners. Cruel glorious own screaming extinction earned. Arriving the random to-day designated your torture extinction—from airplane plummet or nuclear poison—then will memory so many personal crimes comfort, soothe operative into eternity. Important, revered instructor say, "After here, wish top deity a vast pleasure to murder you."

From current today, deserve to die.

Next now, white rodent slide, skid, tumble down drain hole. Feed grinding metal teeth. Gone.

Quote, "I do not see why man should not be just as cruel as nature."

Next now, scream squeal of rodent also gone. Only gush scald water patter metal bin. Glorious wisdom instructor tilt self until both own hand stationed under gush, where hand wrestle each other, wrestle cake of soap, wash clean.

Out black drain of hole, climbing white whisper of steam. No squeal, no animal odor. White rodent erased.

Dispatch
Sixth

Begins here sixth account of operative me, agent number 67, attending initial today structured compulsory education session. Public education institution ████████. Middle level ████████. Homeroom ████████. Dated current now. For official record, American education facility devoted humiliation and destroy all self-respect out native youth. Conspire to degrade all dignity. Calibrated tasks assigned to destroy all self-esteem.

For official example, purpose lesson titled "Junior Swing Choir" many potential brilliant youth compelled sing song depicting precipitate remain pummel head of operative me. Complain how both feet too large size for sleeping mattress. Idiot nonsense song. Next sing how past visited arid landscape aboard equine of no title. All student compelled, no option.

No baby animal to experiment. No access nitroglycerin. This agent possessing too much respect for teacher ask: Why gorge fatten heads gorging so much useless art and music? No benefit to state!

For official record, moment American instructor display self in classroom door, students no stand and say, all unison one voice, "Greetings, esteemed most revered educator. Accept, please, our gratitude for the wisdom you impart."

Initial classroom session, feet of operative me stand by instinct, mouth say salutation, create full silent in classroom. Instructor eyeing. All student eyeing this agent.

Out rear of classroom, voice, male voice say, "Fuck you, Pygmy."

Other voice, female, say, "Pygmy, you suck ass."

Followed all make laughter.

Could be hand of operative me fling sharp pencil, Shooting Porcupine Dart, *zing-jab*, speed javelin harpooning center of student forehead, render damage brain, if surviving...vegetable.

For official record, cat sister occupy same classroom as operative me. Host sister emanate smoke molten solder smell, finger spotted red burn, shining patches skin scorched. Sister cat eye rimmed irritation, branched blood tunnels exposed, angered of poison solder smoke.

Additional present Junior Swing Choir: Trevor bitch. Also, operative Magda.

Other rooms, hallway, midday eating location, eyes of operative me witness Tibor, Mang, Chernok, Tanek, Otto, and Vaky; all agent attempting shake from heads idiot lyric word of songs, infected worthless language of corrupt Western poetry. Useless American poetry and music no celebrate sacrifice lifetime to preserve state. No herald shining future of bright nuclear weapon, abundant wheat, and shining factory. No, instead most American song only empower to enjoy premature actions necessary for reproduction, grant permission commingle egg and seed among random partner occupying padded rear bench automobile.

American structure education serve primary function introduce partners for reproduction. During sessions, many viable female gaggle, cluster knots around center gossip talk. Batting eye cover skin at direction most symmetrical potential male. Mesomorph male youths, targeted for seed, merely strutting stenched clouds groin fungus infection acquired from appareled unclean athletic supporters.

All must sing nonsense or no allowed college, no advanced physics and training. Force compelled to sing how yearning for location on top arched spectrum of light wavelengths created by precipitate. Exact song expressed Judy Garland, woeful martyr, slaughtered pawn of capitalist entertainment machine combined pharmaceutical complex.

If no sing, all youth condemned into poverty. Denied possible advancement and self-realization.

During "Junior Swing Choir," compelled stand so make fence, layered several rows human fence, driven sing brainwash song, operative Magda tilt from behind this agent. Magda mouth into ear of operative me make whisper, say, "Comrade?" Say, "Commence you phase first of Operation Havoc?"

Mouths of operative me merely fashioning lips shape of lyric words, no sing, say in return, "No, comrade."

In order gain training organic chemistry or nuclear particle flux statistics, must engage too many idiot ritual: paint picture, volleyball, make waltz, craft poetry, participate dodgeball, scream idiot songs, torture violin or piano using many false note. Total most today, many useless task. Worst ever torture to watch youth wasted.

Worst wasted time, how idiot song occupy head of operative me. Song involving how dangle in side-to-side motion from distant solar body, next convey illuminations of lunar body to domicile contained in glass vessel...idiot song drive all useful knowledge from head. "Junior Swing Choir" a conspiracy oppress American youths, create them future slave workforce, singing million idiot song during labor of frying meat burgers. Dunking fried potato of France deep in bin boiling fat.

Whisper of Magda say, "Operative Chernok by current now seeded often several American female." Say, "Operative Mang planted embryo own host mother."

Magda insist phase first must soon complete. Say, "Comrade, seeded you own host sister?"

For official record, effect worst—idiot song flush from head of operative me most irregular verbs Mandarin Chinese. Erode all knowledge Portuguese. Idiot lyric overwhelm understanding of advanced field equations calculus. Overpower and devastate to oblivion stored memory to operate Iranian-manufactured Khaybar KH2002 medium-barrel assault rifle. Crowd until no longer recall how many rounds per minute capable firing Ukrainian Vepr assault rifle.

For official record, only inside head of operative me, say, *No. This agent no fornicate atop cat sister.* Only instead report own status, in retort say, "Comrade agent thirty-six?" Say, "Mindful of own mission, carry you current now American embryo?"

No retort. Merely bellowing crowd American prince and princess, perfumed in misery of third-world labor—sewed bright garments. Trouser shivering of plastic telephone apparatus, await reply. Other youth thumbing keyboard to build English printed words, convey instant message.

Clouded within fog of idiot singing, whisper of operative Magda say, "No, have received no American seed..." Say, "However, formulate major plan to acquire."

Fence row, erected immediate front of me, back shoulders and neck of host sister. Smell melted lead metal smoke. Hair gathered to plummet down sister backbone.

From behind, Magda say, "Priority first, must each generate American anchor baby." Whisper quote famed radical anarchist Mikhail Bakunin, say, "'The passion of destruction is also a creative passion.'"

In front, trouser of cat sister vibrate. Hand of sister snake to retrieve telephone from own pocket. Eyes look message words printed in English. Replace telephone into trouser.

Magda whisper, hot breathing at ear, "Must quick, Pumping Rabbit Maneuver, *squirt-squirt*, plant seed into her!"

Quote, "The passion of destruction is also a creative passion."

Next now, cat sister swivel neck to eye operative me. Craning neck to eye backward over own shoulder, host sister say, "Pygmy?" Say more loud to battle against singing noise, say, "Trevor Stonefield just texted me..." Utilizing own hand, cat sister finger fast contact own forehead, contact sternum, contact left deltoid, contact right deltoid—superstition gesture—hand describing shape of fake torture man burdening sticks. Fashion eyes wide, say, "Watch out for Trevor in dodgeball, okay?"

Dispatch Seventh

Begins here seventh account of operative me, agent number 67, seated among sleeping chamber of host sister. Domestic structure Cedar. Suburb community ███████. Date ████████. For official record, night of today host cat sister absorb all light.

Host cat sister apply face with black paint, all layer black, surround mouths, eyes, to make white tooth shine bright, white eye appear vast blinking minstrel show. Arms and legs appareled black blouse and trouser. Feet, black shod. Black blouse feature neck of turtle. Sister eye rest on own eye reflected mirror mounted in own hand.

Eye of operative me steady consume sister gesture and progress to disappear own face. Current today, this agent repeat sit balanced edge on host sister bed, mattress pile with blanket. Animals of brown weave all smile. Silly animal.

Outside window of sleep chamber, night of today. Sky no display orbit moon. No speck distant solar systems.

Next now, door swing from healed in wall, display pig brother.

Remain eye rest on own black face in mirror, host sister say, "Geez, do you ever knock?"

Host brother say, "You putting on your makeup for the dance tonight?"

Sister smooth paint along edge of eye. Face sideways to mirror, eye cornered to witness self-reflection.

Pig dog brother rest eye on operative me. Host brother foot

kick bed, say, "How about you, Pygmy? Up for some fresh seventh grader ta-tas?" Half face collapse as one pig dog eye squeeze shut. Make wink eye. Say, "Get you some fine, hot sweater meat?"

One hand mounted mirror. Opposite sister hand, tips smeared black from paint, cat sister say, "Mom and Dad conk out yet?"

Pig dog brother say, "You overdose them again?"

Host sister spread both hands along sides of face, plow hair backward, flat. Contain strands hair utilizing loop synthetic latex. Hands loop tight again, repeat loop latex band until hair remain pulled flat to skull. Cat sister withdraw sliding compartment out front of cabinet, full inside laundered apparel, engineered for support mammary. Plus stored there many inside trouser sewed sheer nylon for tight encase sister groin and buttocks. Yellow color. Printed many genitals of daisy plant. Sister say, "Pygmy?" Say, "You going out for the Model United Nations?"

Pig dog brother say, "Not Pygmy, here." Fisting own hand to make small slug, impact deltoid of this agent, host brother say, "The Pygmy only ever wants to hunt the fine fun bags..."

Mouths of operative me say, "Define?"

"Fun bags, you know?" say host brother. "Paw patties, gobstoppers, rib bangers..."

Mouths of operative me say, "Define?"

Host brother cup both own hands hovering over own pectoral muscles, bend fingers to squeeze invisible, flex fingers during shut eye, during tongue muscle wipe own perimeter mouth, say, "Sweater meat!"

Cat sister gut innards of sliding compartment, tunnel excavate groin apparel until retrieve black fabric. Knit many knot head cover, crafted black fibers of sheep. Host sister stretch knit head cover so encase hair, rendering all own head black color. Torso, black. All sister black as night of today. Black as outdoors. Out cabinet among mammary binders, retrieve black apparel crafted shape of hands, tight to fit of fingers inside, render hands black.

Host brother fashion own hand shape of revolver gun, aim finger to direction this agent, say, "Trust me, Pygmy, the Model United Nations is social suicide." Fashion half own mouth so make smile, with eye rest on sister, pig dog say, "The only deal more lame than Model United Nitwits is the frigg'n science fair!"

Cat sister make small parade to window of sleeping chamber. Black encased hands grip frame of healed window, slide to make open. Enter chilled oxygen, mating call cricket. Sister step black-shod foot exit window until straddle sill. Outdoors foot rested on tree limb, outdoors hand gripping tree foliage, half exited, cat sister revolve minstrel face to rest eye on this agent and pig dog brother. Say, "Did you steal it?"

Pig dog say, "Catch." Arm of host brother swing forward until hand blossom, fingers spread open to release object. Green object fly, wet shining object flash green, describe arc across sleep chamber, skirt inside roof, trajectory degrade until, *smack-grab*, snatched by blackened hand host sister.

Host sister say, "Enjoy those bodacious titties, boys."

Inside head of operative me, quote villain emperor, accomplished huckster Adolf Hitler, quote, "Great liars are also great magicians."

Next then, sister slipped beyond window, black absorbed into night of today. Leaving cricket mate noise. Sister shadow poured among shadow, lost in no light. Next now, engine automobile usual operate by host mother, starter solenoid engage, fuel combust, drive train propel twin-beam headlight.

Expel from curb. At traffic halt indicator, headlight veer to follow right-hand corner.

Pig dog tilt own torso until head sprouted outdoors window, holler into black oxygen, say, "You shouldn't be driving." Say, "You ain't even old enough to bleed!"

Quote, "Great liars are also great magicians."

Green object tossed then caught, theft object shining bright with wet—green glass crafted artificial human prosthetic eyeball.

In chilled black oxygen, twin shining red light of automobile tails gone.

Dispatch
Eighth

Begins here eighth account of operative me, agent number 67, attending student mating ritual located darkened sports arena of education facility. Night of today ██████. Ritual song perform ██████. For official record, American family invent infinite plentitude absurd labels for christening female offspring.

For official record, face skin this agent dosed liberal generous amounts fragrant Listerine.

During mating ritual cloaked dim interior arena atop floor of basketball wood, against din of music encourage premature random sexual reproduction, pig dog brother make finger straight to indicate females ranked along opposite wall. Across distance, give introduce. Assembled females of middle school, could be rowed for execution firing squad, eyeballed by youth males. Host brother poke finger toward, say, "...hooters...knockers...balloon bombs...butter bags..." Say, "Rib cushions...party pillows...chesticles..."

Hovering within proximity, operative Tibor, neck of that agent bruised chain of purple hematomas, select bruise wreathed with indents biting teeth. Operative Mang also sport necklace purple hematoma. Also neck operative Ling gnawed by phantom teeth.

"You want to do science fair?" say pig dog. "You can start by inventing some super-megastrong Spanish fly and dosing the cheerleader squad." Continue, make straight finger, say, "Blouse bunnies...fun bags...lactoids...speed bumps..."

Rowed among opposite females, operative Magda present self for male inspection.

Host brother say, "Milk makers . . . devil dumplings . . . floatation devices . . ." Pig dog abrade fingers together so generate slip quick, *snap-pop*, fast sound matched to rhythm of mating dance music.

Occasional male student approach female, request mutual gyrate to demonstrate adequate reproductive partner, fast gyrate to display no cripple. No genetic defect to bequeath offspring. Demonstrate coordinated, plenty vital to provision impregnated female throughout gestation period. Provision subsequent offspring until matured. Females flaunt dermis and hair to depict viable vessel for impregnate, paint face so appear most symmetrical. Best likely produce frequent alive births.

Around most-dark perimeter of arena interior pace Trevor Stonefield, clear-yellow bully nose remain folded sideways, asleep against own face cheek. Lurking.

Pig dog brother slink plunge hand to depth of own trouser pocket, produce small cylinder. Hand bring cylinder to own face, where host brother mouth expand to display tongue muscle. Finger of hand compress top surface cylinder, release pressurized into own mouth orifice canister jet menthol stinking mist down length of tongue muscle. Host brother say, reek breathing menthol, "Okay, Pygmy, you be my wingman . . ." Say, "Who shall we cut from the herd?"

Mouth of operative me say, "Whom." Making finger of this agent straight, indicate across dim arena to location Magda. Agent 36 brown eye rested on pig dog. Magda remain require impregnate so fulfill phase first Operation Havoc.

Trevor bitch linger, walk circle, stalk so remain predator eye rest forever upon operative me.

Pig dog cast own eye to Magda, curl own lip, say, "No doing." Say, "That one looks like a botched thirteen-year-old sex change."

Could be fist of operative me lash, *bang-bam*, Pummeling Kangaroo, to silence host brother. Instruct more humble.

"Besides," say pig dog, "I hear she bit the throat out of Reverend Tony."

Devil Tony.

Trevor bitch menace more proximate. Curtain blond hair nearing enough bring reek cologne. Glaring electric bolt out blue eye.

Next then, pig dog departed, swagger bisect arena, approach females for proposition.

Next now, operative Metro venture proximity this agent, deliver mass thick quantity American dollar. Covert delivery. Followed operative Tanek, in secret bestow paper monies extracted out food plate at Sunday worship shrine.

Hands this agent stash legal tender concealed own trouser. Feet of operative me make small parade to follow pig brother. For offer sacrifice this agent to reproductive partner. Eye cast on ranked females, inside head, quote this agent, quote honored rebel, steadfast revolutionary Che Guevara, say, "I know you are here to kill me." Quote, "Shoot, coward. You are only going to kill a man."

Feet of operative me present best appearance before prospective partner, female Mongoloid featuring brachycephalic-shape skull, small nasal aperture, and projecting zygomas. This agent fashion pleasing mouth of smile, trumpet clear voice to compete music din, say, "Respected potential reproductive vessel, request engage preliminary foreplay ritual prior genital coitus..."

Mongoloid female, absent brow ridges, backward tilt own

face so display nostrils, nasal aperture to this agent. Female hand lift long tress own hair where lay down front of chest, hurtle hair backward over own shoulder. Nostrils flared, female say, "Shove off, freak."

Next then, this agent approach negroid female characterized by mesocephalic-shape skull, wide nasal aperture, and receded zygomas. Hand of operative me extend, open to female, this agent say, "Specimen female, permit perform mating dance prior generate human embryo?"

Mouth of operative me assure equipped adequate chromosome so no burden society care for deformed monster progeny.

Respected negroid female fashion mouth to display frown. Rotate face to one side, then other side, repeat rotate to make head meaning "no."

Next then, this agent venture near Caucasoid female featured with dolichocephalic-shape skull, large brow ridge, and receded zygomas. Feet of operative me rooted stance, breathing distance away female face, this agent own hands akimbo, fist planted atop each own iliac crest, say, "Esteemed Madam Fun Bags..." Say, "Request demonstrate superior anatomy as condition to receive generous deposit of alive male seed."

Next now, *swipe-pow*, Caucasoid female slap hand impact face cheek of operative me, sufficient violent so generate blood glow, swell outline of female digits on face skin of this agent.

Noise of slap hand impact reverberate repeat, reaching every corner dim arena. All female young casting eye so rest upon operative me. Madam Sweater Meat. Madam Jugs. Madam Party Pillows. All breathe whisper behind cupped hand. Make straight finger poked direction this agent. Madam Blouse Bunnies rest eye on this agent, open painted mouth and insert most long finger so to mimic produce vomit. Madam Chesticles say, "Fuck'n loser..."

Eyes of operative me scrub arena to discover pig dog, only host brother engaged mating ritual dance. Abrading genital area against genital area of operative Magda.

Next then, backbone of operative me detect pressure, feel muzzle stamp of Colt Detective Special DA snub-nose .38-caliber, alloy-frame version, two-inch barrel, poke this agent spine junction thoracic vertebra twelve and lumbar one. From behind, male voice breathe whisper into ear of operative me, say, "You and me, Pygmy, in the parking lot, right now..."

Voice of Trevor bitch. Stench cologne.

Snub nose squeezed between clear-yellow bully and this agent, make small parade perimeter dark arena, past Madam Butter Bags, past Madam Hooters, until door label "Exit."

Could be legs of operative me spring, spin, kick, *zing-blam*, Launching Leopard, scatter revolver out Trevor hand, shatter wristbone. This agent only patient until gain solitude out-doors, swing open door so access chilled oxygen, faint illumi-nate mercury vapor security lamp. Macadam storage field of idle automobile. Night of today. Pressure of snub nose remove off backbone so this agent able revolve self, face to rest eye upon attacker.

Security lamp reflect silver-barrel double-action revolver. Trevor bitch say, "Don't try anything funny..." Shake cur-tain of clear-yellow hair away sides own face. Bully hand turn revolver redirect until snub nose pressured to location own heart muscle, bracing .38 Special so shoot own chest, Trevor bitch say, "You tell anybody what I say, here, and I swear..." Trevor finger click trigger, hammer cocked.

Trevor say, "You breathe a word, and I'll kill myself."

For official record, happening absolute truth.

Bullet aimed so destroy own self, Trevor say how enamored strongly of this agent. Since violated by force, men's spa room of shopping mall. How never so experienced such passion. So used and taken beyond own person control . . . Own boundaries expanded . . .

Clear-yellow bully spout many statement proclamations. Declare dedicate to dying adoration this agent. Say many such affections. Gush generous words of appeal. "You won't have to say 'hi' at school or anything." Say, "I'll understand."

Trevor typical normal Caucasoid male . . . dolichocephalic skull, narrow nasal aperture, long nasal root height—prior folded flat against face cheek. Sagittal crest measure within normal variations. Digits of hand grip revolver to own rib cage, digits squeezed white of no blood. Bitch voice drone and drone. Cologne pollute night oxygen. Ritual music leak from interior sports arena. Bitch voice remain drone.

For official record, ears of operative me no actual affording attention. Merely await pause, Trevor to breathe inhale.

After time, mouth of Trevor Stonefield stop moving. Silent. Revolver barrel remain dimpling chest of own shirt, aimed to destroy own heart muscle. Blue eyes starving for reply.

Mouth of operative me say, No love. Say how instead, bully suffer merely Stockholm syndrome. No able accept how possessed of no power, helpless, so reaction bonded alliance with aggressor. Form identity with oppressor. Typical victim psychology mechanism. No doubt Trevor own father brutalize so generated stronger bond father and son. Too threaten to risk hate. Cruel thrash become replace genuine gesture of familial affection. Violence synonymous love.

Voice of operative me fashioned soothing, inform Trevor bitch merely exists as manufactured product cruel society, so entrenched no aware how motivated by personal history.

Trevor Stonefield no responsible, merely animal pawn. Ignorant puppet. Victim Western system.

New now, this agent fashion pleasing mouth of smile,
trumpet clear belly laugh. Tell clear-yellow bully to rejoice.
Many additional thug available to brutalize him into future.
Multiple infinite opportunity seek damage from battering.
World offer always strangers to enjoy sadism, exert domi-
nant.

Operative me say Trevor no actual love this agent. Instead,
bitch merely thug bully for loving brutal power. Say how all
tortured slave in secret romance with master.

Illuminate of security lamp glisten alloy of revolver barrel.
Glisten slow crawl shining water bleed out eye Trevor bitch,
blue eye both bleed water. Face twisted, issue sob of breath
while entire skeleton tremble. Twist of mouth burst open to
say, "Couldn't we just *go steady?*"

For official record, the deity model only correct behavior.
All must do unto fellow being what the deity does to all.
Night of today, this agent further earn future own screaming
cruel extinction.

This agent say, much apologize, but cannot waste more
seed within Trevor anus. Must retain so impregnate future
offspring. Say, "Is no personal."

Next then, feet of operative me pivot. Legs step one ahead
the other, the other ahead, the other a stride until walking
departed Trevor and bullet. Own face pointed no look backward, throwing own voice over shoulder in parting, this agent
quote honored rebel, steadfast revolutionary Che Guevara, say,
"'Shoot, coward. You are only going to kill a man.'"

Feet of operative me remain walking. Breath locked within
lung of operative me, awaiting for impact of bullet.

Dispatch
Ninth

Begins here ninth account of operative me, agent number 67, regaining host residence subsequent attending student mating ritual. Return via public transport bus route ███████. Transfer route ███████. Walk final segment to follow public byway ███████. For official record, backbone of operative me no penetrated by revolver ammunition Trevor Stonefield.

Along returning journey, encounter frequent memorial honoring American battle warrior, great officer similar Lenin. Many vast mural depicting most savvy United State war hero. Rotating statue. Looming visage noble American colonel. Courageous, renown of history, Colonel Sanders, image forever accompanied odor of sacrificial meat. Eternal flame offering wind savory perfume roasted flesh.

Further official record, host domicile structure harbor own share increasing intrigue.

During this agent pick primary door lock resident domicile host family, eye of operative me witness shadow having rapid motion. Silent shadow edge perimeter host family landscaped property. Shadow leap so grasp lower limb *Castanea dentata*, gain purchase until lift shadow self to next high limb. Hidden foliage, shadow slide more height along *Castanea dentata* main trunk. Next then, perched adjacent window of cat sister sleeping chamber.

Shadow so stealth could be operative Chernok. Engage covert camouflage as operative Ling. Perhaps operative Tanek violent attempt to inflict seed.

Could be twin leg of operative me spring to perform Flying Tree Squirrel, *zoom-grab*, arrest progress of shadow and prevent from imminent fertility attack upon asleep host sister.

Only next now, shadow present self amid ribbon illumination from lunar satellite. Pale watery illumination. Revealed no malice entity. No housebreaker. Instead, arm and leg snaking within window revealed as cat sister, appareled black blouse and trouser, face smeared black paint.

Inside head of operative me, quote ideology despot, fiery orator Leon Trotsky, quote, "Insurrection is an art, and like all arts has its own laws."

Burdened, slung to carry over shoulder, sister totes fabric sack weighed with mystery cargo. Initial sister disappear within window. Next now, sack of cargo conveyed into sleeping chamber. During all procedure no sound twig snap, no rustle foliage. No neighborhood canine cry out. No electric fixture illuminate interior sleeping chamber.

Quote, "Insurrection is an art, and like all arts has its own laws."

When calculation position lunar satellite, taking account season, place hour at 1:07 with twenty-four-second margins for error. For official record, host family domicile remain dark. Sister window slide until healed in wall. Remain outdoors this agent to accomplish pick lock, gain entry.

Dispatch Tenth

Begins here tenth account of operative me, agent number 67, recall former practice offensive attack exercise ▮▮▮▮▮▮. Battle gallery ▮▮▮▮▮. Headquarters ▮▮▮▮▮. Combat rehearsal dated back many year. For official record, repeat recounting here formative history of operative me.

For reinforce early lesson training of operative me.

Depict here standard battle gallery, layered mirror to cover all one wall. No window. Cement floor sullied often with blemish ancient bloodstain. All operative present for the practice of Flying Hyena, *lash-pow*, single leg sweep thrust. Operative Tanek. Operative Bokara. Operative Pavel. Especial operative Pavel, agent 43. Battle gallery reverberate grunt of exertion during combat. Pack thud noise bone battering impact against opponent muscle. Gallery reek stenched operative perspire, stink chlorine bleach having ghosted ancient history floor bloodstain.

Foot of operative me, sparring kick, sweep air to shatter skull of operative Magda. Sweep thrust during Magda evade, return own Flying Hyena to stomp ear of this agent. Leave this agent stunned, ear listening ring sound.

Under no shadow of fluorescent illumination, electric hum, grunts, thud blows landed, operative Tang spar operative Chernok. Operative Sheena spar operative Ling. Operative Pavel battle operative Boban, agent 11.

For official record, no two operative so opposite spectrum bell curve. Operative Pavel all attempt able foot splinter thick wood plank while kick. Chop hand of Pavel shatter solid brick concrete, single *swing-bash*, Elephant Stomp brick so become dust. Every sparring, operative Pavel manifest Whirling Wolverine: head butt, hip check, poke eye, spin until become blurred. No agent parallel.

For official record, operative Boban combat entire opposite talent, perpetual hesitate. If land any blow, Boban immediate say, "Sorry." Kick groin, say, "Sorry." Bite windpipe, say, "Sorry." Inflict Lashing Lynx, *slash-scratch* to opponent, operative Boban say, "Sorry..." If suffer any blow, impacted Boban, agent 11 crumple to floor, arms wrapped so clutch own rib cage, eye squeezed to retain water. Out clenched teeths, Boban forever say, "Good hit, comrade." Knotted around own pain, say, "Top congratulations." Forever skin spotted as Dalmatian dog, bruise hematomas. Hopping stride with lame leg. Face skin secured shut with sewing stitches. Boban forever absent plethora front teeths.

Pavel, top of class. Boban, ultimate most low.

Pavel, brilliant wolverine. Boban, suffering pigeon.

Boban squeal as baby swine during Pavel knuckle punching, swift kicking. Agent 43 so grind agent 11 flat, next then more flat against floor so spreading red most recent stain blood. Pavel pound utilizing foot heel. Pile drive utilizing bent knee, dropping entire own weight to pulverize with bony knee. Operative Boban, mouth leaking blood, open wound scalp leaking blood, Boban remain forever say, "Sorry...sorry...sorry." Say, "Excellent hit, comrade."

All Pavel blow splashing up many spray drips of blood, during operative Pavel remain pounding, remain stomping.

Operative Magda launch elbow slam to craft ruptured eye of operative me. Operative Tibor twist neck of operative Tanek. Visible all operative layered in mirror wall. All wearing naked foot, wearing black color uniform trouser with blouse, belted with holster of regulation pistol. Wearing grim face of combat, all operative remain spar during floor become more slick coated splash of Boban blood, agent 11 mouth swollen, no tooth, say slurred, words vomit of red saliva, say, "Exceptional hit, operative Pavel."

Operative Magda heave battering shin to meet genitals of operative me, flood awareness full suffering pain, spur desire contents stomach to project. Reproductive weapon of operative me hammered with agony, mouth of this agent say, "Well-done, comrade." Say, "Injury put in jeopardy entire future generation operative."

Next now, operative Pavel cease Flying Hyena stomp to carnage of Boban. Pavel stance above fallen agent, balloon own chest with deep inhale. Operative Pavel rooster crow, say, "Ha-ha!" Brandish deadly hand chopping oxygen too fast able eye to witness. Shake own fist at roof. Rooster crowing, say, "Bring me more bones to break!"

New now, door no remain healed in wall. Door of battle gallery swing so display best-accomplished attack instructor. As required, all sparring cease, with unison all operative announce: "Greetings, esteemed most revered educator." In single unite voice, say, "Accept, please, our gratitude for the wisdom you impart."

For official record, Boban no speech greeting.

Pavel foot kick into rib cage of operative Boban. Repeat boot. Repeat repeat boot until Boban eye cover skins flutter, lips whisper say, "Greetings, esteemed most revered..." Voice fail.

Instructor bow head.

Operative all bow head.

Acclaimed instructor make small parade to penetrate gallery. Respected instructor revolve head to cast eye, rest on all combat operative as individual. Step deeper into battle gallery, hands clasped behind own back, jawbone firmly set. Stance tapping shoe repeat against floor, tapping only noise in gallery, tapping until wrapped all heartbeat into unison. Next then, shoe stop. All heart stop.

Top revered attack instructor swivel head to cast eye on operative Pavel. Projecting own chin, instructor say, "Savor your most high status, comrade." Say, "Simple to decide you as supreme among total this operative class."

Bloodied hands folded behind own back, operative Pavel balloon chest, make small bow with head.

Eyeing matted, blood mess crumpled of Boban on floor, trembling buttocks of agent 11, much wisdom instructor offer own hand, say, "Grant me your pistol, comrade Pavel."

All operative issued regulation Beretta nine-millimeter, semiautomatic, double-action, recoil-operated, hip-holstered, loaded fifteen-round reversible magazine. Muzzle velocity 2130.3 feet per second. Operative Pavel release safety strap own holster, withdraw pistol, grant over to instructor.

Receiving nonglare Beretta, matte-black finish, top accomplished instructor say, quote benevolent ruler, stern dictator Augusto Pinochet, quote, "'Sometimes democracy must be bathed in blood.'"

Respected instructor direct pistol aim upon crumple Boban, click trigger to cocked.

Operative Boban, eye squeezed, body curled, clenched, balled tight around own heart muscle. Nostril sniff to retain water. Uniform matted blood.

Operative Pavel fashion mouth to make curling smile of pleasure. Display every shining white teeth. Smile wide as to compress Pavel eye into slits.

During event witness, fellow operative breath locked inside lungs. Skin layered sweat growing chilled.

Next now, pistol discharge. Loud retort. Smoke of stink rising.

That same current now, Pavel smiling head explode. Bullet violate skull, exhaust soft gray contents, spattering mirror wall. Spattering operative Magda, operative Chernok, operative me. Warm blobs gray sponge, former thinking machine of operative Pavel.

Pavel skeleton buckle, spiral until heaped garbage proximate to weeping Boban.

Brass metal shell casing of ammunition arc ejected out pistol, trajectory degraded until strike concrete floor, bounce— ding sound, ding sound, ding.

All much valued education of Pavel, all skill and experience, every memories, dreams for glory, regrets, affection and loathing, education of history events and trigonometry equation, entire personality with identity, all of these blasted. All skill and talents. Past and future. All meticulous plan and training and practice. Pulverized and shattered. All former joy and sorrow made steaming gray meatloaf, evicted from skull out exit wound.

Respected attack instructor flex knees, stoop so hand able retrieve brass shell casing off floor.

For official record, announce instructor, the state requires no epic hero. No strive achieve personal celebrity of spotlight and applause. Lectures instructor, the state desires best ideal perform as mediocre. No gain attention showboat. No buffoon. Best effort so occur average. Suppress climbing ego. Become ordinary. Invisible.

Required to erase own self. Otherwise state will do so.

During lecture, instructor rotate own head to put face upon

individual operatives. Contacting eyes of each. Next then, cast own eyes on rubbish of Pavel. Cast eyeball on quaking mass, bloody flesh Boban.

On concrete floor, agent 11 shiver. Cower. Single drop yellow urine roll stripe from trouser cuff of operative Boban. Both knee pulled to own chest, squeezing self most small as able.

Acclaimed instructor make pistol arm straight at shivering spine, backbone of operative Boban. Next then, barrel flash. Blam. Smoke.

Quote, "Sometimes democracy must be bathed in blood."

Last blood escaping agent 11. Dying final breath, lips fluttering, operative Boban whisper, say, "Best congratulations, revered instructor." Exhale own precious life to say, "Most excellent shot..."

Exploded drops Boban blood... burst gray blobs of Pavel brilliance... chilled sweat trace slow crawl down face cheeks of operative Magda, operative Tanek, operative me. Knees of this agent automatic flex, stoop so hand able retrieve brass metal casing of ammunition. Finger chilled. Cradled in palm of operative me, casing shell retain tiny warmth.

Dispatch
Eleventh

Begins here eleventh account of operative me, agent number 67, attending this today structured compulsory education session. Participate combat among student public education institution ███████. Forced battle to list English alphabet letters which comprise typical vocabulary word. Spelling war staged auditorium ███████. Dated current now. For official record, all American youth become casualty, already slain attempt letters to build *coordinate* or *transpire*. Six youth destroyed from battle against word *separate*.

All American student dismissed from battlefield, relegated into seats of audience, able only witness remainder word skirmish. Displayed onstage no one except operatives, Magda, Ling, Chernok, Oleg, Bokara, Mang, Tibor, Tanek, in addition this agent.

Stern foot operative Mang take step to stance of microphone, focus of stage spotlight, say repeat word given from instructor, say, "Steatopygia." List alphabet, say, "S-T-E-A-T-O-P-Y-G-I-A." Bow head, repeat say, "Steatopygia."

Out audience issue massive huge moan. One voice male scholar say, reverberate throughout auditorium, say, "Get this bullshit *over* with!"

Chorus other voice, male and female voice, say, "Yeah." Say, "Call a fucking draw, already!"

Seated below footlight of stage, rank of esteemed instructor rifle many volume book, dragging finger down page searching next word for ask. Other acclaimed instructor make finger straight and press to own pursed lips, exhale hissing sound to signal quiet. Other revered instructor tilt chin almost touch microphone, say, "Next contestant . . ." Say, "Would you please spell 'retromingent'?"

Onstage, operative Magda taken stance at microphone. Arms folded behind torso, feet apart, parade rest stance, Magda say, "Esteemed instructor, most grateful with full respect if would repeat word . . ."

Say instructor, "Retromingent."

Eye of operative Magda fixed no blink into high glare of spotlight, no blink, no bleed water, say, "In most great due respect, great instructor, regret to correct most esteemed instructor pronunciation." Say, "Actual correct version pronounce 'retromingert.'" Proceed list exact alphabet of word.

Heckler of student audience say, shouting, say, "Somebody pull the fire alarm. Get us *out* of here."

Ranked next beside this agent, whisper into ear of operative me, operative Chernok say, quote extreme king sheriff Benito Mussolini, say, "'It is humiliating to remain with our hands folded while others write history.'"

Trevor killed, casualty of word *aneurysm*.

Cat sister retired from battle over word *coagulopathy*.

For official record, during evolve past 6.21 hours competition, team of instructors forced often retreat to school library, retrieve additional volumes listing English word. Top respected instructor cup hand to shield microphone, pull own mouth to sideways speak other fellow instructors, say, try inaudible say, "For cry'n out loud . . . I'd like to go home someday." Say, "Let's blow this punk out of the water."

Pig dog host brother, destroyed from elementary word *phthisis*.

Venerated instructor crack thick volume text, eyeballs

scrub, hunt page, search most difficult word, contain most number alphabet.

Ranked awaiting word, operative Oleg insert elbow against rib cage operative me, tilt head nodded to indicate female student, say subject youth absent menses since five week. Request say how many American ovum enjoy the seed of this agent?

Next now, best important instructor screw eye tight to rest on operative Tanek. "Please spell 'oocephalus.'"

Operative Tanek incline so place mouth adjacent microphone, say for celebrated instructor please to utilize *oocephalus* embedded context sentence.

Honored instructor wrap own face within spread finger both own hands. Exhaust oxygen of lungs one prolonged blast. Eyes squeezed, tilt face at microphone, say, "Here's your sentence, kid... 'Oocephalus is one tough motherfucker to spell.'"

Wrinkle stream weak laughter filter among student audience.

Operative Oleg repeat drill elbow, dig into rib cage operative me, say, "Where possible acquire lederhosen apparel?"

This agent ask repeat.

Tanek list alphabet, O-O-C-E...

Oleg recruited participant Model United Nations. Explain multiple student mimic delegates world governments, all nation, assemble to battle question current global issue. Deliver oratory. Calculate vote. Castigate with resolution sanctions. Operative Oleg assigned represent delegate Germany. Chernok feign Italy diplomat. Magda act behalf France. Bokara figurehead nation Spain. Ling, the corrupt evil despotic Ireland. Oleg allege no American student desire represent Western nation, American youth strictly aspire serve as delegate third-world government, racial ethnics, marginalized former colonies subjected imperial powers, striving achieve self-ruled. To follow, disco dance of all nations so demonstrate mutual affection world peace. Exchange personal body fluids.

Tanek list alphabet, P-H-A-L...

Even as observing, breasts so many female youth swelling, bigger cup, inflating blouse from pregnant. For official record, this agent no impregnate. No recruited delegate to Model United Nations. Become merely target for attract eyeballs lovesick sodomite Trevor Stonefield.

Tanek list alphabet, U-S.

Organized horde, lauded instructor, all assert vast moan at victory operative Tanek. Audience mob erupt profanities, slouch sliding deep inside seat cushions. Focused typing tiny message keyboarding personal telephones. Twist own arms so read hour on wrist clocks.

Insistent pointed elbow of Operative Oleg, repeat wedge rib cage of this agent. Oleg repeat say, "Lederhosen?" Say operative Tanek to mimic delegate Portugal. Operative Mang ape delegate Great Britain.

Quote, "It is humiliating to remain with our hands folded while others write history."

Feet of this agent approach stance microphone. Tilt head back so mouth more near for catch voice. Hands wring pole so telescope microphone most low level where remain on top head of operative me. Arms folded behind. Parade rest to await barrage English word.

Illustrious instructor, finger pressed to page inside volume, lips slowly create sound of word, pronounce fragments in manner of reading child. First able reading child. Instructor say, "Pheo...chromo...cy...toma." Cast eyes onto stage and repeat say, "Pheochromocytoma."

For official record: Ha. Effortless facile word, simple to list alphabet. However eyes of this agent witness audience, breath locked inside waiting lungs. Audience eyes no blink, fingers twisted in cross of superstition, praying this agent fail. Cat sister plus all student craving operative me to stumble listing alphabet.

Mouth of this agent say, "P-H-E-O..."

If flounder alphabet, build of myself hero. Martyr. As Moses and Fidel Castro, to liberate fellow youth to freedom, improved lives.

Mouth of operative me say, "C-H-R-O-M-O..."

Shout single voice, male youth beyond footlight, say, "Spell it right, asswipe, and you're a *dead* fucking pygmy."

Mouth of this agent say, "C-Y..."

For official record, no impossible shouting death threat originated from renowned instructor.

Next now, sail object up from audience, dark mass emerges out stage footlights, slam down, *bam-pow*, hit downstage boards and slide to arrive beside feet of this agent. Sailing projectile object: English dictionary.

Mouth of operative me complete, say, "T-O-M-A."

Dull rumble build. Stage lights, oxygen crowded pelt, raining down various object. Dictionary. Thesaurus. Thundering impact stage boards. Novel *Jane Eyre*. *Catcher in the Rye*. Song volume lyrics Junior Swing Choir.

American youth enjoying to commence riot.

Next now, siren of fire alarm begin shrill.

Dispatch
Twelfth

Begins here twelfth account of operative me, agent number 67, on arrival religion propaganda distribution outlet of city ████████. Outpost community ████████. Date ████████. For official record, devil Tony repeat in absent.

For official record, worship shrine of community offer tanning box where supine nude so become scarred beneath artificial solar body. Offer infinite variation beverage extracted dried coffee bean. Offer gallery ranked machines purpose build muscle through resistance training. Every thus, in addition forgive moral transgression of individual. By today of next week to offer feature movie rentals. Drop box of rental returns stationed beside poor box.

Plaster fake dead man bleeding red paint. Reek of burning paraffin. Stink of genitals various plant life. As prior, all male compelled bind neck in knotted banner of decadent silk fabric. Female all cover head. Seated to control bellow machine, ancient parrot, Mrs. Lilly. Lips of operative me greet, say, "Best hello to sacred animated corpse." Say, "How decayed is glorious brain on this today?"

Responding aged parrot twist wrinkles so fashion smile, say, "Fuckoff,youlittleforeigntwerp."

Host father mount altar so stance beside bin empty of water. Bin drained subsequent operative Magda attempted to murder drown under hands devil Tony. Water absent, and empty bin ringed around with circle yellow tapes, outlining edges of bin tapes printed English words *CAUTION*

CAUTION CAUTION CAUTION... Within walled sides of bin, to mark former level of water, sides stained in tidal mark of blood red. From position immediate beneath man bleeding paint, host father, vast breathing cow father say, "You'll be happy to hear that Reverend Tony is recovering nicely." Say, "The fine paramedics of our community report that he suffered something they call a 'submucosal throat hemorrhage' brought on by his screaming..."

Devil Tony buried bottom of water, anchored tight within clutching arms of operative Magda. Screaming sound, next then screaming bubbles, next then screaming blood.

From seated neighboring this agent, voice breathe whisper. Cat sister say, "Hey, Pygmy, want to do me a big, big favor?"

From distance across worship shrine, Magda eyeball this agent and host sister.

Whisper of cat sister say, "It's about the Model United Nations next week." Say, "Nobody wants to be the United States... will you?"

For official record, this agent requested to represent American nation on council floor, service on security council, create policy.

Whisper scented of solder smoke, melted lead connecting circuits sister mystery project, whisper say, "Special favor?" Host sister lift hand, fingers straight as for pledge or vote, say, "Swear, I'll owe you, big-time."

On condition this agent act as delegate on behalf United States will host sister be indebted. So vast appeal.

Cat sister say, "Plus, Ms. Matthews will give you extra credit in Social Studies." Say, "Plus, we're having a Dance of World Peace after."

Perhaps as redeem favor, fulfill obligation, could host sister open vagina for deposit seed of operative me. Permit this

agent complete task phase first, Operation Havoc. Perhaps—
hope beyond all hope, dream beyond impossible—cat sister
consider make ritual dance with this agent.

Continue sister say, "I'm going as Swaziland. United Nations is exactly like Halloween except more political." Say,
"My brother's going as Ceylon. He figures since nobody knows
jack about Ceylon he can just make up stuff."

From distance across shrine, lips of Magda form words,
mouth silent quote magnetic giant, appealing fascist Benito
Mussolini, say, "The fate of nations is intimately bound up
with their powers of reproduction."

To cat sister, will agree . . . only if host sister allow this
agent to accompany along during next secret foray. Apply to
face of operative me black paint, apparel black, attend secret
mission to venture through window during next planned escape night of today.

Cat sister say, "I don't know . . ." Rotate face to one side,
then other side, repeat to make head meaning "no." Say, "It's
kinda illegal . . ."

From distance, breasts of operative Magda appear more
volume, more round, crowding sweater. By ominous magic
agent 36 breasts rapid inflated.

Quote, "The fate of nations is intimately bound up with
their powers of reproduction."

Cat sister say whisper, "You have to swear." Say, "Swear to
fall down dead if you tell." Host sister say, "The truth is . . . *I'm
a spy.*"

Face of operative me fashion arced eyeballs surprised,
mouth gaped open with slacked jaw. Say this agent, "No."
Whisper say, "A spy?"

Cat sister tilt face forward, tilt backward, repeat to make
head meaning affirmative. Say, "Now, swear."

Lips of operative me expectorate into palm of own hand, extend salivate hand to cat sister. This agent agree to represent American nation only if sealed hand shaking.

Waiting long now, then now, then now cat sister rest eye on pool salivate. On final now, extend own hand covered spittle. Host sister embrace, clasp entwined fingers to encase pocket of slippery warm fluid between.

Dispatch
Thirteenth

Begins here thirteenth account of operative me, agent number 67, on council chamber floor, Model United Nation, conducted suburb of city ████████. General assembly session ████████. Date ████████. For official record, operative me acting as delegate United States, appareled appropriate traditional American wide-brim, ten-gallons boy of cows head covering, coated reflective sequins of colors blue, white, and red. Foot shod boot associated profession boy of cows. Borrowed of host mother. Skinned ostrich. Otherwise appareled black fabric tunic printed English words "Property of Jesus," sewed so appropriate fit vast North American obese endomorphic body type. Hemline tunic flair loose flapping knees of operative me.

This agent appointed acting general secretary for oversee Model United Nation.

For official record, fellow delegate display colorful costumes represent own varied native lands. Lady delegate Malawi adored harem trouser pink gauze, so thin no conceal black color bikini thong within. Buttocks cleaved traditional black butt floss. Despite Caucasoid, male delegate Gabon adored dashiki, many insect molded black plastic, fake houseflies sticked to own pale face skin painted latex spirit gum. Caucasoid male delegate of Qatar draped torso bandolier countless rounds machine gun ammunition, fist of young Caucasoid blond hair, lifted as Black Power salute.

All Caucasoid youth delegate of third world, adorned

necklaces fake animal teeths, straight hair fashioned cornrows, fashioned dreadlocks, or ratted style Afros. All Caucasoid with straight narrow nasal aperture, bred genetic trait to shed European precipitation, today seated behind desk nameplates: GUYANA, PERU, GAMBIA, MYANMAR, EQUATORIAL GUINEA. Fanning own selves utilizing palm fronds. Whipping cords own shoulders, shoo no present tse tse flies. Complain much over malaria. Discuss quality fresh drinking water. Compare infant mortality rates.

Suspended from roof, board of scores. From wall, bottomless basket woven of cord netting for inserting balls. Golden floor polished basketball wood, no permitted tread dark-soled footwear fearing heel mar, skid mark. Same arena location as held ritual mating gyrations.

Lady delegate Kiribati straddle leg gentleman delegate Tuvalu, both nation representative draped immodest skins of artificial animal tiger, ragged loincloths, drawing ballpointed pen Senegal symbol fake tattoos high on inside skin surface each the other pale thigh.

Lady delegate Nepal festooned transparent veil across face, breast concealed within brassiere shimmering gold coins. Shimmy gyrate hips. Gentleman delegate Bhutan feature animal bone inserted through topknot of hair, loins girded grass skirt, brandish spear. Other lady delegate adorned coconut brassiere. Other, sari. Other, kimono. Other gentleman, diapered as Gandhi. Other, Nehru jacket. Turban. Woven conical coolie hat. Sashay in plaid pleated kilt.

Delegate each court breeding partner. Delegate fulfill reproductive imperative.

Form trade alliance. Forge peace treaty. Negotiate lower barrier tariff.

Other delegate waving headdress crested feather style Las

Vegas showgirls, seated at nameplate Brazil. Other delegate stumble down aisle council chamber, tripping on hemline own burka. Other delegate carry walking staff topped human skull, own face streaked colors white, black, yellow war paint.

Normal tribal tattoo American youth, multiple piercing nose and lip and ear, only this today appear appropriate. Accessory to costume.

At podium, this agent gavel, *pow-pow*, gavel, *pow-pow*, gavel, *pow-pow*, to bring general assembly to order.

Operative Chernok as delegate Italy sucking the earlobe of lady delegate Venezuela. Oleg appareled lederhosen. Operative Ling fondling buttocks of lady delegate Mexico.

From stance atop stage Junior Swing Choir, stance at podium, piping voice of operative me in vain request world congress come to order.

Operative Magda cover head under black beret, carry long baguette bread, penciled ink across own top lip, black line so suggest mustache. Magda approach stage, stance at feet of operative me, casting eye up to this agent, Magda say, "Bonjour, comrade, urgent must have discussion regarding colossal topic." Eyes of that agent leveled with knees of operative me, Magda tilt torso so able wield bread baguette, batter legs of this agent. Clubbing so, say Magda, "Immediate." Say, "Impending event at stake."

For official record, that same now, cat sister approaching, hips wrapped snug around with fringe red shawl knotted to one side of waist, fringe sway, whole one leg bare almost so groin exposed. Wrapped on top head, host sister adorned with red turban, dangle gold metal loops from each earlobe. Piled atop turban, artificial banana, pineapple of plastic, rubber grapes, fake apples, towering crown inedible fruits. Swing thighs, sway fringe, balancing head covered of fruit, cat sister arrive beside operative Magda at foot of stage. Host sister lift both hands, brace sides of fruit so able cast eyes up at podium, this agent. Cat sister say, "Trick or treat!" Say, "Guess who I'm supposed to be..." Same now, say, "I'm *Cuba*."

Operative Ling oral cavity engaged oral cavity Turkey.

Magda eye bleed water, single path of drip down own cheek. Smudge pencil line of black mustache. Say, "Please."

Next now plastic pineapple of cat sister commence vibrate. Sister burrow fingers between bananas, retrieve small black apparatus. Personal telephone. Eyes rested on buttons, say, "It's Sri Latke."

Say Magda, "Sri Lanka."

"Whatever," say host sister, thumbing button keyboard, say, "Sri Lanka says Afghanistan has the biggest crush and could totally jump the bones of Morocco." Eye fix English text screen, telephone, say, "And this is so wild...the Falkland Islands are breaking up with New Zealand and heard from a reliable source that Namibia has scary dick warts..."

Say Magda, "Excuse, but request Cuba no profligate gossips." Say, "Assume comrade Cuba assigned member seat."

Say cat sister, "Sit down, yourself." Remaining eye at telephone, say, "Honey, this isn't just any gossip." Say, "This here's global world politics!"

Lady delegate Zaire fingers toy blond cornrows hair, trickle laugh to display healthy teeth, extend long smooth muscle of neck.

Projecting own voice most tone sorrow loaded bitter contrition, this agent say, "As official empowered representative for the citizen peoples of the United States..." Say, "As first duty, compelled before this august body of nations to apologize..."

Remain fellow nations kissing. Nations keyboarding instant massage. Nations plugged with music into both own ears.

Hands of operative me remove ten-gallons head cover, clasp between both hands, hug to own chest, and say, "This American nation duly recognizes itself as the evil tyrant source of all world misery, the most selfish ignorant superpower..."

Lady delegate Romania cup hand behind own ear, wave other hand so to silent fellow delegate. Gentleman delegate Poland pluck music plugs out own ears so able listen.

Enlarged loud through microphone, amplified voice of operative me say, "United States consist of merely 4.6 percent the world total population yet consume over 75 percent global energy resources."

Gentleman delegate Czech Republic cease fondling coconuts of lady delegate Haiti.

Operative Magda make small parade so mount stage, stance at behind shoulder of operative me, breathe whisper at ear of this agent, say, "Utmost crucial to initiate dialogue, comrade."

During assembly chamber gaining quiet, voice of operative me remain loud, lips of operative me tilted so make contact metal mesh surface of microphone, voice amplified loud, say, "Fellow momentous delegates, request assembly buttocks attain appropriate locations."

Voice say, shout, male voice, "Fuck you, Uncle Sam!"

Stance below podium, delegate draped folds of sleeping fabric sheets, pattern with many smiling animal, silly animal clutching floated balloon, sheet draped to form toga, stance at foot of stage delegate masked behind video camera. From face eclipsed with camera, male voice muffled, say, "I'm shooting a video called *Nations Gone Wild*." Toga delegate lower camera to display face. Revealed as pig dog host brother, head wreathed artificial foliage laurel colored glittery metallic gold.

Pig dog delegate say, "Guyana just flashed her rack for me!" Say, "For a banana republic, she's totally awesome!"

Stance at elbow, Magda clutch "Property of Jesus" tunic, give tug, say, "Demand grant attention, comrade."

Pig dog delegate say, "Pygmy, little man, pass some declaration making this session clothing-optional." Say, "I gotta nail some footage of Ethiopia." Say, "That little vixen is smokin' hot!"

Distant perimeter assembly chamber, delegate vixen exchanging saliva with tongue muscle Palestine. Both nation locked mutual clutch so hands vanished within blouse and trouser of other.

Gentleman delegate Jamaica distribute cakes baked, odoriferous wealth chocolate pieces, fragments walnut and hashish.

Delegate Algiers arrive transport on person elaborate hookah crafted brass metal, reservoir water sloshing, trailing plethora octopus arms tipped brass mouthpiece. Algiers instant swarmed many delegate cramming octopus arm inserted mouth, sucking bubble through water during Algiers ignite brazier. Spiral corrupt smoke out brazier, out exhaled delegate lungs, stinking reek *Cannabis sativa*.

Operative Magda fill breath into ear of this agent, say, "Most top priority must communicate..." Push shoulder this agent using freshly expanded party pillows, blouse bunnies, rib cushions.

Pig dog mount camera to own face, say muffled behind lens, say, "Yo, Canada!" Say, delving returned depth of crowd, pulled by camera focus into delegate mix, while vanish, say, "Jiggle me those bodacious northern hemispheres!"

Amplified voice of operative me, announce against din telephone ding, bubble hookah, flurry voice, slap hand delegate Sudan impacting face cheek delegate Jordan, eruption laughter, burst scream, this agent announce against fog cannabis smoke, say, "Present this today for discuss topics of global important." Continue say, "Must address increase temperature atmosphere, enlarged ozone hole, decimation Amazon forest, must stem extinction giant panda, halt religion persecution, nuclear proliferation, sexual disease pandemic."

Hemline lifted delegate appareled burka, below hemline revealed clear-yellow body hair legs. Burka flap so display paramilitary combat boot issued desert operations, male size fourteen double-E laced so girdle such dense leg fur.

Fellow delegate merely continue chatter, grope, eat hashish cake. Delegate Russia slide stealth hand within own tunic, hand emerge around bottle sloshing clear liquid vodka. Fellow delegate clamber as infant bird, all head tilted backward, teeth yawned open at roof while Russia splash vodka down each swallowing throat.

From foot of operative me, this agent extract boy of cows boot, swing boot to batter podium, heel pound lectern so microphone transmit as great sound boom. Over speakers, deafening boom. Splitting ear boom. Crashing boot heel, boom sound, boom sound, boom, until general assembly no able communicate among delegates.

Boot boom until floor assembly chamber silent.

Until Magda whisper retreat. No tug tunic.

Until voice of operative me stand alone.

As representing vast pile United States, this delegate announce apology. Announce immense regret how American nation contain merely 3.6 percent total world population, however consume 95 percent total world energy resources.

Express sorrow how seven from every ten American citizen suffer morbidly obese, blind plus amputated of every arm and leg. Vent remorse over wealth American economy constructed atop backbone African slaves. Genocide native peoples. Exploitation ethnic immigrants. Subjugation female citizens and sacrifice conscripted males into slaughter of imperialist warfare.

As speaking for vast American citizens, this delegate announce motion to sanction United States. Announce this nation to immediately cease exporting degenerate mass culture. Immediately disband constituted states, from current now create result fifty petty fiefdoms. Nation of Montana. Nation of Arizona. Nation of Florida. Fifty battling insect kingdoms.

In continuing, announce to forgive all overseas debt. Additional to pay sanctions amounting to all hoarded gold money Fort Knox toward gaining affection of esteemed third-world nations. Plus to make available own cherished American children, ship overseas as lifelong chattel slaves, gesture shown of goodwill.

Floor of general assembly silent, reek only vodka, cannabis smoke. Listening ear.

Expressing much vitriol, this delegate proclaim former United States to summarily execute by slow torture—bloodletting or cooked alive atop bonfire—all existent own leaders, present and former, on every levels. From vile corrupt federal president to evil puppet maid of parking meters. All to be tortured before corpses dragged through public street and head mounted pointed pike.

Next now, panting declarations of operative me, moment required pause to draw another next inhale; at that silence, Magda interject.

Perhaps microphone adjusted too loud. Perhaps assembly so quiet. Magda voice only whisper, but explode so reverberate every corner of chamber. Magda say, "Insist hear, comrade..."

Broadcast so resonate throughout all delegate, Magda voice say, "I am big with child..."

Delegate Argentina, delegate Japan, delegate Myanmar retaining cannabis smoke locked in lung, exhaust smoke into bursting guffaw. Next now, whole entire chamber filled guffaw. Flood guffaw upon guffaw, great waves buffeting stage. Stink breath of ridicule eroding operative Magda, laughter consuming operative me.

General assembly erupt laughter roar. Conflagration laughter.

Next now, delegate appareled burka reaches hand to grip own hemline. Delegate lifts hem to reveal within: trouser leg cuffs rolled to knee, display torso, expose face of Trevor Stonefield. Reveal tucked behind buckle of waist belt: Colt DA snub-nose .38 caliber, alloy-frame version, two-inch barrel. Trevor hand gripping trigger Detective Special.

Into ear of operative me whisper Magda, quote pugnacious visionary Vladimir Lenin, heroic autocrat, say, "One man with a gun can control a hundred without one."

Muzzle flash. Loud retort. Stench gunpowder smoke.

Same current now, head of delegate Sri Lanka explode.

Second muzzle flash, head of delegate blond cornrows Zaire explode. Next then, East Timor fez explode. Egypt turban. Feather headdress Brazil explode.

All much valued education of nations, all cultures and legacy, every event history celebrated as holiday, children of future. Contribution to civilization. State ideology, language, laws, all of these blasted. All aspiration and crimes. All opinion and prejudice. Pulverized and shattered. Concept of the deity, ethics, native aesthetic. All best ideals of nation made steaming gray meatloaf, evicted from turban or Afro or jeweled crown out exit wound.

Delegates paralyze. Delegates flee screaming. Other delegates remain laugh, belch vodka, or cough bloodshot-eye cannabis smoke.

Pig dog record pogrom through camera. Cat sister ducking fruit head, bananas, and plastic pineapple so shelter beneath delegate desk, keyboarding telephone summon police. Magda in refuge behind podium, debate if burdened with fetus able execute Leaping Hyena, Monkey Mash, or Launching Leopard, *fly-blam*, for neutralize attacker.

Quote, "One man with a gun can control a hundred without one."

During all, Trevor snub-nose remain erase fellow youths. More explode heads.

Eyes of operative me cast on cargo within Magda blouse, enlarged bosom, and this agent say, "Comrade, actual in truth impregnated?"

And Magda, agent 36, fashion mouth of half smile, wipe bread baguette to mop mustache with eye water, black ink saturate white bread. Soiled bread. During all, tilt Magda face forward then back, face forward then tilt back, repeat to make head meaning "yes … yes … yes."

Dispatch
Fourteenth

Begins here fourteenth account of operative me, agent number 67, recalling former marched parade event in celebration ███████. Reviewed by supreme high commandant ███████. Assembled military force combined infantry and artillery home nation ███████. Occurrence parade dated back many year. For official record, repeat recounting here formative history of operative me.

For reinforce early best important training of this agent.

Depicted here vast apparatus for national defense, stretch length central boulevard, filled one curb to opposite, ranked solid many battle tanks thunder rolling steel treads. Battle tank Leopard 1A5 sourced Belgium. Tank Type 99, 96, 59 sourced People's Republic of China. Infinite row, tread clanking stone pavement. Tank Zulfiqar MBT sourced Iran. M48 Patton sourced Lebanon. K2 Black Panther tank sourced Republic of Korea.

Boulevard great capital city, lined citizens cheering behind cordon rope. Lavish paved sideline central boulevard, press solid many mouth shouting tilted backward, throwing cheer so display only teeth. Many hand froth sky, whip blue sky countless number proud national banners.

Blue sky, no cloud mask against admiration of sun.

For official record, all generation operative drilled participate. Operative Tanek. Operative Magda. Operative Mang. Follow strict squad leader signal utilizing baton. Leader command forward march, standard eight-to-five stride, cover five yard each eight step. Standard stride 22.5 inch. Matched speed battle tank, artillery rockets.

Ranked between infinite battle tank, parade 90-millimeter caliber Kanonenjagdpanzer antitank artillery, sourced Germany. Impressive barrel 152-millimeter antitank gun type ISU-152 sourced former Soviet Union. Also Soviet 2S4 Tyulpan self-propelled mortar measure 240 millimeter of caliber.

March along imposing majestic field grenade launcher. Momentous vast acreage self-propelled assault gun Rooikat 76 sourced South Africa, field gleaming weapons, extensive rolling plantation thrilling steel metal and ammunitions pass in review.

Planted row after row such total power aspiration, operatives march forth as proud harvest. Prepared for reap.

Citizen crowd clutching behind rope, witness assortment antiaircraft Oerlikon thirty-five-millimeter twin cannon sourced Switzerland, prompt citizen swoon. Chest balloon much inhaled pride. All faces flash cheering teeth. All hand brandish whipping flag.

Out of horizon roll black river foot soldier, many ten thousand so form black flicker of infinite left trouser legs stride forward. Black pulse as infinite black right leg trouser take stride. Horde soldier dense so assume single black column. Row beyond number. Soldier beyond able count. Black pulse and pulse and pulse while so dense leg together stride, so infinite arm shoulder rifle. Great harvest shining ripe soldiers, vast marching acreage flash as division leader order face grandstand for review.

Helmets without end, inspired howitzer, field guns, siege cannon, and noble battle tank stretched out one horizon until the opposite, always progressing, no able enemy this state resist.

Approaching review grandstand, venue hosting boundless brilliant leaders this state, unlimited great wisdom national statesmen, approaching march operative Oleg, operative Chernok, operative Vaky. All stride exact 22.5 inch. Operative heel immediate before clanking tread battle tanks. Boot of operative forever shadowed looming at back, tower above operative, FV101 Scorpion tank sourced Botswana.

Amid din so numerous proud cheering citizen, hollering, pressed behind cordon rope as runners after marathon race so many million miles now no able break finish line. Panting citizen strain against cordon, hand grip rope, tilted forward until faces within parade. Citizen teeth and hair press among passing light autocannon. Faces dodge progress self-propelled mortars.

Within din cheering, voices say, "Oleg." Say, "Oleg, look here!"

Before short distant, female citizen clinging cordon rope screaming mouth exact same mouth of operative Oleg. Citizen female, blue eye mirror eye of Oleg. Female say, "Darling, my Oleg!"

Flanking female, citizen male also strain behind cordon, fanning hands for attention. Male brandish stuffed bag, sewed of artificial animal fur, bag stitched with pair black button eye, stitched with nose and mouth to fashion miniature fake bear. Citizen male flailing small bear, say, "Oleg." Scream say, "You're alive!"

Rank and file marching operative Tibor, operative Ling, operative me steady approach deranged male and female citizen. Parade dress uniform. Issued sidearm Beretta nine-millimeter, semiautomatic, double-action, recoil-operated. Polished black boot. All stomp unite. All stride as single stride.

Lunatic female duck own head beneath cordon, violate

rope, crawling along road pavement stones by hand and bent kneecap, say, "Wait." Lunatic male follow below rope clutching imitation stuffed bear. Male citizen display hair duplicate to operative Oleg. Duplicate same Caucasoid nasal bridge, prominent zygomatic arch above each cheek. Same pallid Oleg complexion. Deranged male throw self into street, say, "We've found you."

Eyes all operatives cast at baton of squad leader, mimic tempo signal. All stride 22.5 inch. Thunder clank battle tank treads immediate behind operative heel. In front, judging gaze unbounded state superiors to witness from grandstand.

Lunatic male and female grovel pavement stones, scramble hands to bridge gutter, stumble to walk upright. Keening wail. Wielding stuffed bear. Deranged male and female dodge moving steel mountains, Challenger 2 battle tanks sourced Oman, skitter between chewing treads M1 Abrams sourced Somaliland. Demented citizen overcoats flapping open. Citizen hands reaching. Outrunning battle tank T-84 Oplot sourced the Ukraine.

Next then, deluded male and female apprehend operative Oleg, panting oxygen, gripping black dress uniform. Lunatic female, eye bleeding water flooding own face blind until water sheet own cheeks to chin, say, "They took you for testing." Clutch Oleg, stamping lunatic pursed lips so contact many locations operative Oleg face, say, "They took you, and said you were dead."

Deranged female clutching Oleg. Deranged male clutch female, tugging to remove out rank and file state operatives. Extract from entire parade.

For official record, operative Oleg produce great resistance. Launch counterattack, sweeping leg to make *zing-blam* Leaping Hyena, foot battering lunatic female. Fist smiting deranged male. Agent 68 make elbow *bam-cram* Punching Panda. Fashion head-butt *bam-wham* Ramming Ram, additional while continue march, covering five yards with every eight stride.

Next now, lunatic male flaunt fake bear. Expose black eye crafted button. Stitch mouth. Citizen male exhibit sewed artificial fur bear, say, "We brought Wolfy." Say, "You remember Wolfy..."

Lunatic female straining so contain battling limbs of Oleg. Leaping Lizard. Hitting Hound. No body able advance until body Oleg advance. All operative frozen. All cannon and battle tank grind until total halt.

Vast muscular might entire enormous state approaching official annual review. Eminent top statesmen await.

Same now, pallid blue eye of operative Oleg land frozen on fake bear. Oleg feet no stride. All limb no fashion Punching Panda.

. Male and female deluded citizen envelop operative, encase black dress uniform within layers lunatic arms circling around.

Oleg halted, squad halted. Squad halted, battle tanks halted. AMX-30 sourced Venezuela halted. Model 1877 siege gun sourced Italy, halted. Steel clank out treads, rumble, looming progress shadows along pavement, halted. Silent. Vast apparatus of state power and might clogged from lunacy single male and female. Brutal steel metal armored plated tanks, treads stop roll, cease rumble for reason two demented citizen silly embrace single youth on path.

Crowd citizen roped aside, halt cheer. Hand halt whipping flags. Blue sky left silent so only witness foolish mouth of aberrant female clutching inhales while grinding self so fused to idiotic male and victim Oleg. That operative, agent 68, much assaulted with affectionate gesture, heavy violated utilizing caresses.

Vast mighty display military machine power, straight driving phalanx, total interrupted.

At present location between two distant horizon, all halted. Spread acreage infinite soldiers shouldered with bazookas, with loins girded pistols and ammunition, remain merely witness. Crowd silent citizen witness.

Next then, prudent stride squad leader among rank and file frozen operative. Adroit squad leader arrive so to grip nape of citizen male neck, *pinch-squeeze* until male collapse. Repeat same effect on lunatic female. Both deranged citizen fallen crumple heaped to pavement, squad leader command Oleg, say, "Atten-hut.

"Operative," say squad leader, trumpet for all parade so register, say, "Behold two diseased cellular units of the state." Say, "Witness two infectious bodies."

Lunatic individual threat as cancer, contagion to the state, spread dangerous illness so destroy all. Must excise. Heal state. Purge infection.

Eye of operative Oleg, blue eye merely remain rest upon fake stuffed fur. Black button eyes and stitch mouth, fallen among pavement stones at beside deranged female.

Sage squad leader say, "Present arms."

Obsession lunatic man and woman, restraining entire yearning streaming phalanx state military machine. Misguided affection-deranged citizens, choking righteous purpose whole vast device state power.

Squad leader face filled blood glow, repeat say, "Present arms."

Operative Oleg release holster strap, withdraw Beretta

loaded fifteen-round reversible magazine, muzzle velocity 2130.3 feet per second. Oleg blue eye empty as blue sky. Chilled blue of no cloud.

"Reject damaged dangerous organism," say squad leader.

Lunatic female lift own shoulder, propped own elbows so rest eye on Operative Oleg. Entire whole structure of female pushing deranged face so more close. Same mouth. Same eye. Irrational mouth open, say, "My sweetness..."

Idiot words.

Same current now, muzzle flash. Loud retort. Stink gunpowder smoke.

Face demolished. Dangerous words eliminated. Contagion all vented out exit wound from behind of skull where foolish blood saturate artificial stuffed bear. Imitation fur sponging escaped blood. Sodden. Fur bag of button eye, stitch mouth, filling red with blood glow.

Eyeball astute squad leader observe corpse lunatic female, leader squat so clasp ankle cadaver, drag until corpse reside lengthwise along gutter of boulevard. Boot squad leader, kicking cadaver to gutter, shrewd leader say, quote grand ruler, magnificent chieftain Benito Mussolini, say, "'War is to man what maternity is to a woman.'"

Next then, lunatic male stumble backward, spring so upright feet, flee. Mental ill male tunnel path digging with elbows, driving with own knees so escape, possible able spread insanity infection.

Operative Oleg drop to assume sniper crouch, stretch one own arm as brace, steady hand of nonglare Beretta, matte-black finish so able sight diseased target in distant. Receding target clamber among audience crowd. Muzzle sight steady. Tracking target.

Next now, muzzle flash. Loud retort. Smoke. Impaired brain lunatic male, hair so mirror hair Oleg, yellow hair explode, cascade hot gray meatloaf surrounding citizens.

Crowd explode splitting ear cheer. Acclaimed squad leader signal, wielding baton so indicate new march pace. Step size of thirty inches. More fast six-to-five speed, cover five yards with six strides. Making more fast toward eventual victory. More speed abandon failure misery of past history. Improved progress each thirty inch, thirty inch, thirty inch into new shining bright future.

During march, eye of operative me cast on passing stranger woman nose same as nose this agent. Behind cordon rope, stranger mouth mirror mouth of operative me. Name of operative me choked back within throat strange female. Rest on eye identical. Inside head, voice of operative me say, in secret say, *Please...* Say, *Must no attempt rescue.*

Eye of operative me warn stranger woman yearning forward, display same ears. Caution stranger male fanning hand for snag awareness this agent. Stranger man offering same face as operative me, same nose and eye, same exact mouth and color hair. For protect possible reproductive source, this agent turn away. Fashion scowl with brow, cast eye opposite direction.

Next now, next now, next now many ten thousand boot striding. Tread stomp face stuffed bear. Row after row operative stomping boot down atop face stitched black button eyes, saturated blood of dead lunatic. Each stomp wring blood out stuffing, press fur more flat. Each row, bear squeezed more dry. Chewed below tread of battle tank, grinded on pavement stone until vomit stuffing, repeat so bled dry, stomped empty. More small, more small particles until small bear never exist. Erased.

Soaring so control sky, Rafale C fighter jet sourced France. Parallel stripe many JAS-39 Gripen fighter jet sourced Sweden. Pregnant of glorious AIM-9 Sidewinder missile.

Boots marching print tread, track printed blood down boulevard.

Proud boots treading gray matter, stomp stuffing, until history neither distant nor recent past no longer exist.

Quote, "War is to man what maternity is to a woman."

Boot of operative me, entire whole generation this agent stride to direction far horizon, march step, march step, marching five yard every six stride toward distant vanishing point.

Dispatch
Fifteenth

Begins here fifteenth account of operative me, agent number 67, seated subterranean chamber designated purpose family Cedar observe television viewing appliance. Subdivided community residences border major metropolitan area ██████. Date ███████. Recumbent aboard large upholstered bench crowded many cushions, accompanied host pig dog brother so analyze documentary video recorded during resolution Model United Nations. Evade numerous telephone contacts American television network program ███████.

For official record, drooling jackals of American news media pacing outer perimeter this residence. Outdoors swarm many journalist hyenas, equipped camera, capable ruthless satellite broadcast. Hovering parasitic vultures. Patience relentless pack buzzard.

Pig dog brother review variety news images current distributed. Scrolling different evil network affiliate, all display weeping citizen subsequent Model United Nations. Show corpse dead delegate Brazil, covered white fabric, fabric stained red. Revealed as Brazil merely reason towering headdress rainbow parrot feather sprout beyond one edge white shroud.

Within head of operative me, quote enlightened prophet, regal martyr Richard Nixon, say, "When news is concerned, nobody in the press is a friend—they are all enemies."

For official record, additional reside aboard bench cushions vast breathing cow, host father. Twitching chicken, host mother. Dual host parent unconscious splayed wide limbs spread, neck muscles lolling heads loose until rest own shoulders, lips loose, trickling long ropes translucent saliva. Unconscious, breathing prolonged liquid inhales, loud sputtering exhales.

Host brother hard elbow sleeping father, cram aside so cushions able accommodate brother and this agent. Pig dog brother keyboarding buttons layer surface small silver-color box. Point small end of box direction television appliance, continue keyboarding. Nothing occur. Glass face television viewing appliance become dark, no issue image. Continue dark.

Host brother invert silver box, finger open tiny latch so expose small gold-color cylinders. Pry cylinders free, say, "Thanks Mom..." Small cylinders pinched between thumb with index finger, brother shake near touching shut eyes of host mother. Shaking cylinder in chicken mother asleep face, host brother say, "Thanks for leaving us your dead batteries."

Then now, make small parade to arrive sleeping chamber, where, normal today, host father sleep atop mother. Pig dog brother bend knee so able reach arms below mattress host parents. During kneel, penetrate both arm deep below mattress, extract wide, flat box. Plastic box molded of vivid color blue, stenciled images vivid red, vivid yellow, and color orange. Image striped tiger animals so leap to fly through ring-shaped inferno. Other image, male appareled decadent Western formal wear, coat of tails and tall hat, flogging whip at nothing. Other images classic comic figure featuring white paint on face, comic red nose, ludicrous oversize apparel. Comic figures tossing spheres in circle so all suspended.

Host brother fashion face of half smile, tap box with index finger, say, "This used to be *my toy box*."

Hands of brother manipulate latch, lift so top cover open

on hinges, reveal interior cluttered numerous small missile, plethora diminutive bomb. By smooth appearance, colors pink, yellow, white, probable cast plastic or latex rubber. Some missile ribbed many flutes. Missile chased with bands many bumps. Some bomb short mortar shell, boasting wide girth. Other bomb stretched long, carbine slender. Hands host brother select long missile, artillery shell, gripping by both end, nose and tail, twist same missile two opposite direction. Pig dog twist until seam hidden at midpoint missile, seam appear, widen to reveal threads. Two mated halves of missile twist until come separate. Brother shake one half so cylinders battery emerge out missile.

For official record, hands of operative me select missile, polish so pink plastic slippery to touch. Adhesive in small way to contact fingertips, in slight way surface of missile tacky of history dried moisture. Examining missile, this agent manipulate rotating dial at base. That same now, missile leap with life. Much animated so generate infinite tiny shivering so sudden hand of operative me release, drop quivering missile toward collection weapons, munitions. Feet of this agent lunge to flee before collected total all missile able detonate.

"Good job, Pygmy," say host brother. "You found a live battery." Brother lift shivering missile, twist until seam break, spill out battery. Quivering stop. Remaining hold missile, brother say, "This here's my last year's Christmas present to Mom." With missile, indicate other antitank warhead in box, say, "My sister got her that one." Indicate other missile, huge missile, same size vzor 99 Antos light mortar sourced the Czech Republic, say, "We both chipped in on that one the Mother's Day before."

All munitions mortar and cartridge issue strong odor female pudendum.

Brother assemble broken missile, secrete cylinder battery in trousers. Closing box of vivid blue plastic, say, "For my dad, we bought him a year's premium membership in the Almost Underage Nympho Latinas Web site." Pushing box so returned below mattress, say, "At least this ways we know they're home...and not out looking for trouble."

Make small parade returned to subterranean chamber of television appliance, location host father and mother remain no conscious. Where host brother penetrate silver box, small box surfaced with buttons, insert cylinders, heal hatch. Pig dog brother keyboard box. Television viewing appliance flash, appliance face illuminate image female youth, delegate of Guyana, hands gripping hemline own dashiki lifting so display attractive pair sweater meats. Delegate twist torso one side, then other side, repeat twist so cause adolescent blouse bunnies sway hypnotic motion.

Next now, television display delegate Trevor Stonefield discard burka. New now, head delegate Rwanda consume hashish cake, adorned necklace numerous human teeth, face cheek striped red color, yellow and blue war paints, next delegate head explode. Image paralyze at now when delegate dreams, fears, prejudices, adorations all emerging as pink bubble so burst out side of Caucasoid skull. Delegate mouth remain macerate hashish cake during own entire thinking machine escape.

Pointed silver box at television appliance, pig dog brother say, "Little Pygmy, this tape is my ticket to the big money." Say, "You're looking at a gold mine bigger than the Zapruder film."

Same now, voice say, female voice emerge shadowed doorway, say, "Too bad you intercut with kiddie porn..." Voice revealed as face cat sister, face skin painted black, torso appareled black tunic and trouser. "No news outlet will run underage titties," host sister say, "You'll be lucky not to spend next year sharing a cell with some pedophile."

Pig dog keyboard button so full skull delegate Rwanda vent as vast pink sneeze out ear canal. Keyboard button, and contents delegate accumulate, assemble, leap returned into skull, delegate repeat smiling, eating cake, shaking teeth necklace so dance over naked hypertrophied pectoral muscle. More keyboarding, delegate skull repeat explode. Assemble, explode. Assemble, explode. Advance, retreat. Advance, retreat.

"Stop it," say cat sister. Host sister stoop to examine face unconscious host mother; utilizing finger sister lift eye cover skin of mother. Sister say, "Did you dope them?"

Keyboarding the skulls to explode, the fun bags bounce, host brother say, "All I got to do is cut the boobies." Keyboarding small silver box, say, "At last count, you owe me sixteen roofies."

Next now, cat sister extract small cylinder out own trouser, finger cylinder until one end blaze bright illuminated. Seizing eye cover skin open, host sister aim bright blaze so directed host mother exposed eyeball. There, host mother iris no expand or contract. Cat sister apply two own fingers pressed side mother neck, say, "Her pulse is weak and irregular, dickhead." Bright blaze light begin fade, fainter, fail to dark. Host sister jerk cylinder two direction, finger switch only create no illumination. Say, "Thanks, Mom, for nabbing my flashlight batteries."

Same current now, dark stain liquid bloom on crotch host father trouser. Host cat sister clench own face into fist around own nose, snort small inhale, say, "Dad's wet..." Say, "You plan on changing him?"

"Last time," host brother say, "you yelled that I got talcum all over."

Television appliance depict Trevor Stonefield exercise trigger Colt, expend ammunition. Colt DA snub-nose .38-caliber, two-inch barrel, muzzle flash. Loud retort. Puff smoke. Fez delegate disintegrate. Conical coolie hat atomize.

"Last time," cat sister say, "it was Mom, and I had to change her."

On face of television revealed Caucasoid lactoids delegate Ethiopia, festive jump as delegate lift both hands so adjust bone inserted through own false Afro-style hairdo.

Keyboarding button box, host brother say, "I already got feelers out to six record labels wanting to use my footage in their next hip-hop videos." Say, "No fuck'n way am I dumping this on any network news."

On television appliance, revealed Trevor Stonefield, face curtained at sides clear-yellow hair. Electric-bolt blue eye.

Cat sister say, "That bastard shot me in my pineapple..."

On viewing appliance, bullet discharged of Colt Detective Special trajectory until collide plastic pineapple balanced high atop host sister turban of many fake fruit. Pineapple rendered infinite bits yellow plastic, green plastic. Television image of host sister plummet to assume unconscious heap.

During witness image within television viewing appliance, host brother say, "The word is, old Trevor was a big repressed homo."

Subsequent now, then now, then now, eyes of operative me, host brother and sister merely observe appliance. Speed bumps shake, then fall dead. Chesticles jiggle, then spattered with blood. Gentleman delegate Cayman Islands, catch bullet in forehead. Gentleman delegate Bermuda pierced through breastplate woven porcupine quills.

Host father continue urinate trouser. Silver rope viscous saliva escape mouth corner host mother.

Plunging hand into own black trouser, cat sister produce diminutive mirror. Sister repeat stoop so able position mirror in path nostrils of father. Position mirror below nostrils of host mother, sister say, "They're barely alive, but they'll survive."

Eyeballs remained cast upon viewing appliance, host brother say, "Good luck sneaking past the reporters out there."

Cat sister make small parade to bench cushion where this agent reside. Out trouser, sister produce small jar, twist so remove lid, dip two fingertip into contents. Fingers ladle black paint, hover near face of operative me, cat sister say, "So, Pygmy, you think you have what it takes to make a good spy?"

Sister commence smooth layer black paint so conceal face skin of this agent. Cat fingers contacting about eyes of operative me, tracing paint around lips of this agent. Host sister say, "A spy has to be sneaky." Say, "Can you keep a secret?"

Sister rub skin of this agent cheeks.

Displayed television appliance, dancing devil dumplings delegate New Zealand.

Weapon of operative me expand against limited constrictions own trouser.

Cat sister say, "Can Pygmy hide what he's thinking, like a good spy?"

Displayed viewing appliance, Trevor Stonefield snap pistol new full magazine.

Cat sister stroke black paint down nose of operative me, say, "Can Pygmy here go that ruthless, heartless extra mile?"

Displayed television, diminutive figure this agent crouch behind lectern. Huddled with diminutive figure operative

Magda. Next then, figure this agent launch self toward inside roof, suspended tumble, somersault whole self above ground, spring with both arms off slanted top of podium, sailing wind fast, executing exact *swish-zonk* Lunging Lynx. Sailing Lynx twist so evade bullet spray, zero aiming feet at target Trevor Stonefield, landing both legs Lynx wrapped about clear-yellow head, flex knees so yank Trevor skull off connection atlas, separated at cervical vertabra five near top of spine. Loud pop, instant quick dead. Decapitated. Lunging Lynx ride falling body to floor, Trevor muscle remain twitch, eyeball spread wide with surprise. Same clear-yellow body as violated men's spa of shopping mall. Head wilted on neck, dead. Surrounded weeping balloon bombs spattered red blood. Contortion cadavers dead delegate. Trevor Stonefield interrupted. All anxious, all turmoil and aspiration, all affection and hostility—erased.

Face skin operative me, painted black, deleted. This agent say, "Please, Trevor occurred actual no such terrible individual..."

Already media branding Trevor Stonefield evil demon devil for all recorded history.

Quote, "When news is concerned, nobody in the press is a friend—they are all enemies."

During next now, pig dog brother keyboard so Trevor neck no wrung. All delegate skulls vacuum gray meatloaf contents restored. All returned merry faces. This agent striking podium utilize heel boot associated boy of cows. Auditorium resonate Magda voice: "I am big with child..." Reverberate laughter. Next, brother keyboarding all dead. All alive. All dead. All blood contained. All blood exhausted. Advance, retreat. Advance, retreat. Keyboarding both visions during cat sister exit so retrieve canister talcum powder.

Dispatch Sixteenth

Begins here sixteenth account of operative me, agent number 67, seated aboard public mass transportation routed ▓▓▓▓▓. Transferred of route ▓▓▓▓▓. Transferred of route line ▓▓▓▓▓. Originating transportation route ▓▓▓▓▓.

For official record, during venture to board access current conveyance, vehicle captain rest eye upon operative me and host cat sister, both face skin painted black color. Negroid captain seated so to control steering, accept payment, announce disembark locations along route, captain witness cat sister black paint, say, "What are you two supposed to be?"

Mounting step of conveyance, depositing coinage into receptacle neighboring captain, cat sister fashion wide smile of black-painted face, say, "What?" Host sister contract trapezius muscle so elevate deltoid adjacent ear to fashion shrug, say, "Ain't you never seen a *mime* before?"

Fellow passenger aboard public conveyance, seething broth proletariat, body of labor muscle, boiling cauldron class resentment awaiting only leadership activist brain. Stench perspiration combined inexpensive cologne. Drab appareled colors reflecting various inclement weathers. Trousers color collected gutter rain. Blouse and tunic color soiled cloud. Skin faces fellow vehicle passenger lined from oppression. Required merely this agent mount bold stance atop upholstered seat, so able visible for all present. Perhaps shake upright fist. Next then announce rescue arrived. Stern discipline operative me order command, ferment ignorant proles so sacrifice selves to action of glorious revolution. Prompt fellow passenger mutiny, savage overwhelm vehicle captain until jettison corrupt demagogy, crowd then seize helm—first of public conveyance, second of wayward national state.

"Take your seat, please," say captain, say, "you boarded the westbound number fourteen bus, at the Lincoln Park stop."

For official record, during escape host family residence, host sister and this agent did peer over sill of window, ogle assembly media parasites, ready equipments satellite broadcast and exploit events.

Floating tiny orange light, each trailing smoke of cigarette. Milling horde many journalist predator. Open cups steaming the odor grinded coffee beans stewed with scalded water. Single searchlight flares to illuminate media jackal, appareled uniform jacket with skirt, helmet of rigid hair, clutching microphone, jackal transfixed by flaring light say, "Behind me is the home of the Cedar family, where an unlikely hero has been their resident foreign exchange student..." Say, "Fuck." Say, "Let's try that from the top."

Other searchlight activated, appear additional media buzzard and hyena taken stance before residence of host family. Squinting at light, speaking into glare, uniformed buzzard say, "A foreign exchange student is credited with stopping a gunman and saving the lives of several dozen students today..."

For evade bloodthirsting pack scavengers, host sister vacate residence out window of sleeping chamber, lead this agent grappling foliage, balanced along utmost limb *Castanea dentata*. Immersed deep stealth shadow, navigate limb, second limb, scale trunk so gain access limb provided *Quercus rubra*. Navigate limb, clutching foliage until gain access lateral limb

Juglans nigra, until more removed of vicinity jackal hordes, searching floodlights, and satellite betrayal system.

Ensconced aboard first public conveyance, crowded among numerous elbows and knees American proletariat, jostled sway and jolt, list generated from defects in roadway, flaws vehicle suspension, host sister train own face of black paint, cast eyes upon this agent to say, "Your little friend... France?" Say, "She really knocked up?"

Could be flash-fire-quick instant. *Wham-crack*. Bone elbows spear-pointed sharp bent to soar, Soaring Eagle Double Strike, *bonk-conk*, to left-right temple soft spots of cat sister forehead. Hard hit, *zing-crunch*, to hammer through layer of black hair. Could be, pry. Force open, dry, all friction, all peel of tender membrane until *humpy-humpy* dripping head of weapon wedge room in virgin slit of vagina muscle.

Perhaps only reason to blame affection, hands of operative me not already strike host sister to ground, render cat sister unconscious so able enter with turgid weapon, commit Pumping Rabbit Maneuver, *squirt-squirt*, empty contents testicle awash viable American eggs.

Perhaps true profound affection defined by no entering vagina without consent.

Ensconced aboard second public conveyance, host sister say, "That would be my folks' worst nightmare, me hatching some gross fetus right now."

Appareled black, shod black shoe, cat sister carry fabric sack former encase cushion purpose to cradle skull during asleep on mattress. Sack of white fabric pattern silly animal with helium balloon. White fabric flopping empty, almost empty. Round object sway, swing, small and heavy in bottom corner of sack.

Plunging hand into own trouser, host sister extract jar black paint. Twist lid so unhealed. Fingertip spoon black during cat sister say, "You could use a touch-up." Cat sister fingertips lift toward face of operative me. Sister say, "Close your eyes."

Fingertips Braille face cheek of operative me, stroke smooth, massage. Gentle circle. Greased finger lick infinite tiny licks along lips of this agent. Slippery finger slide width of forehead, tickle eyes cover skin shut tight. Leaving layer black paint. Skin of operative me, whole skin of face rush to meet touch. Nothing in eyes-shut blackness, merely honeyed odor cat sister exhales, sound of host sister voice. Vehicle conveyance vibrate.

Host sister voice say, fingering skin, say, "Your little friend, is her name Marla?"

Lips of operative me revise, say, "Magda."

Ensconced third public conveyance, host sister say, "You're pretty much our compromise." Say, "I mean, I wanted to be an exchange student to Uganda or Tanzania, someplace bitch'n, only my folks were sure I'd get loved up by some bush guerrilla and bring them home a half-breed grandkid." Say, "Their compromise is we sent away for you." Say, "You can open your eyes..."

Cat sister heal own eye cover skins so blind, tilt chin forward so face offered as gift for this agent. Say, "Now, you touch me up..."

Ensconced aboard fourth public conveyance, host sister say, "Nobody needs to go to Tanzania to get preggers around here." Say, "I never told my folks, but a while back Reverend Tony oozed up next to me at youth group and offered his own brand of private ministering." Say, "That's how come I carry my rape whistle..."

Devil Tony.

Digits of operative me explore sister face skin, smooth polish surface each cheek, trace slick edge curved margin mouth, sensation squirming eyeball alive behind eye cover skins, penetrate rim each nostril dipping digits so enter hole smear and retreat, advance and retreat, digit entering nostril more deep and retreat. Coaxing host sister bellow wet *hah-shoo*, sneeze. Repeat spray *hah-shoo*.

Blood glow flood cat sister neck skin, say, "What?" Say, "Are you fucking my nose?"

Negroid captain of public conveyance halt vehicle, activate door so becomes unhealed in metal wall, decree through amplified microphone, say, "End of the line." Say, "All *mimes* please disembark."

Surrounding vehicle, vast night render all hidden. Mating cry of cricket. Frog of bulls croak. Vehicle captain abandon this agent with cat sister along margin paved roadway bordered fence of linked chains, trenched ditch retaining stale water, many invasive plant life. Interrupting fence, gate. Beyond gate, vast field paved macadam.

Arriving vast macadam field, empty of automobile, host sister sprint bending knees deep, knuckles dragging primate posture, shoulders hunched so obscured behind landscaping hedge. Approach building assembled red brick. Sign stationed at entry lettered in English words to read: RADIOLOGICAL INSTITUTE OF MEDICINE. Crouched sister continue grasp fabric sack of skull cushion. Invade sack with hand, extract white card, sized of plastic money card. Laminated card attached anchored spring apparatus for gripping chest blouse pocket of cow host father. Laminated name badge swinging there, giving name Donald Cedar, from orange dot code security level nine. Swipe magnetic strip. American industry typical biological toxin exposure indicate strip.

Host sister brandish card, say, "This is *not* a date." Say, "This is Spy 101 *training*."

Sister walking crouched, stealth follow blurred edge of shadows, eternal obscured from camera security scanning landscape. Host sister say, whisper say, "Think of me as your spy *mentor*."

Arriving entrance of building, splayed so flat against wall of chilled bricks near healed doors, sister plunge hand within fabric sack. Emerge hand cupping green object. Cat sister gesture laminate card at healed doors. Next then handle round green object so aligned lens of box beside doors. Nothing occurs.

Fingering green object so repositioned before lens, say, "We need to get this thing home before my dad wakes up."

Green object, artificial prosthetic human eye crafted of glass. Identical of vast cow father eye. White of eye smudged multiple fingerprint host sister black paint.

Glass eye coated slight adhesive, suggest dried fluid, same sticky surface as plastic missile and mortar owned by host mother. Gloss left dull beneath layer dried proteins, plethora bacterium.

Next now, eye new positioned, locked door slip unhealed. Latch loud clack, sound angry humming. Sister grasp edge of door swing so wide to reveal room within building, fluorescent illuminated hallway, linoleum passage stretched toward direction infinite top secrets. Could be this now, feet of operative me Kangaroo Kick, *wham-bam* sister head, render brain damaged so this agent able access interior of federal government knowledge. Implement Operation Havoc.

Cat sister insert self through unhealed door, hesitate, say, "Since you're still in spy training, you'll be the lookout."

For official record, recall this agent the words of glamorous national heroine, sanctified beauty Evita Perón, quote, "My biggest fear in life is to be forgotten."

Required this agent remain at exterior door, for survey area any possible approaching individual.

Making lunge, host sister impress painted lips against surface lips of operative me. Adhesive black paint bonded for instant. Soft pressured and warm glued together. Next now peeling away until tactile memory. Flavor cat sister. Honeyed smell saliva. Acrid odor solder smoke, melted lead.

Quote, "My biggest fear in life is to be forgotten."

Shake fabric sack, host sister say, "I just have to grab some junk for my science fair project." Fashion face of half smile, say, "How come you *always* smell like Listerine?"

Same now, host sister slide beyond doorway, door returned so healed in wall. Sister ventured to trespass interior, taking laminate card, artificial eye, going delved to harvest unknown mystery. Forsake this agent alone at dark entrance, surrounded by invisible river of chilled wind, mating cry cricket. Night of today. Tongue of operative me licking own lips so able revisit lingering taste of vanished affection.

Dispatch
Seventeenth

Begins here seventeenth account of operative me, agent number 67, on arrival religion propaganda distribution outlet of city ████. Sabbath ████. Denomination ████. For official record, initial public appearance this agent since Model United Nation debacle.

Additional to normal array: Fake statue dead male, fake torture plaster on two crossed stick, fake blood painted red hand and foot...scented genitals plant life...cylinder white paraffin encase burning string, many tiny single fire. This today added pack jackals mass media, baying hounds, circling buzzard, sniffing hyena aim loaded camera, brandishing microphone so gouge eyeball of operative me. Media predator parasites shout demands of smile, look, look second direction, no smile, strobes searing retinas this agent.

Corrupt degenerate American media process image operative me, voice word of this agent preserve as product able reproduce indefinite, utilize to pace insidious marketing memes compelling persons purchase automobile and consume soda. Always purchase and consume.

Starting amidst macadam field where host family surrender protection of automobile, media jackals pursue cow father, chicken mother, pursue pig dog brother, cat sister, and this agent. Hound after until arrive entrance to worship shrine.

Within shrine doorway stance leather mummy of Wal-Mart, Doris Lilly.

Vast breathing cow father, blouse saturated perspiration,

mouth devour and vomit great mass oxygen. Arrival interior worship shrine, cow face flushed dark blood glow, during one hand clutch sagging pectoral location of heart muscle. Chicken mother fluttering own bony claws so breeze own face with chilled wind.

Arrayed along forward edge stage of shrine showcased caskets various United Nation delegate cadaver, prior discarded to nourish worms and bacteria of soil. No longer sway-swing sensuous butter bags. No consume hashish. Lady delegate Zaire current now, adored gown sewed silk, white silk stitched infinite tiny pearls, delegate pallid hands accommodate bundle delicate genitals of tulip plant, fragrant, vivid red, spectral white. Delegate corpse nested deep interior of casket, buoyed aloft padded lining color pink.

Gentleman delegate East Timor grasp football in death, face cheek painted pink paint. Gentleman delegate Egypt eternal posed both hands gripping volume Christian Bible, neck bound eternal knotted silk banner. Lady delegate Brazil deceased hands bondage tied together utilizing necklace beaded, trailing pendant of dead man mounted on crossed stick.

Continued interior of shrine, media hyenas circling. Menacing forest multiple camera, blinding strobe continual sunburst, steady glare provided video recording. Thrust microphones.

Stationed throughout shrine: operative Tanek, operative Ling, operative Vaky.

Present also delegate Uruguay, delegate India, esteemed Madam Fun Bags.

For official record, devil Tony remain no in attendant.

Basted glared heat so multiple camera, listened by so numerous microphone, vast host father vacate seat among family, make small parade so mount worship stage amidst dead casket. Below plaster man bleeding paint. Host father initiate somber voice, say, "As a community we have much to mourn today . . ."

No present cadaver Trevor Stonefield. No in attendant family clan surviving Stonefield.

Mounted worship altar, host cow father say, "Not long ago, a young man came to us, dirty, ragged, smelling like the dung cooking fires of his primitive homeland." Say, "This boy came to us as an orphan, a product of a dismal, backward culture mired in the failed social experiments and misguided politics of long-ago history." Say, "This stunted child, crusted with scabs and stooped with rickets, with a stomach bloated from malnutrition and sparse, thin hair, he arrived illiterate and confused . . . And no, don't get ahead of me here; this child was not our savior, Lord Jesus Christ of Nazareth . . ."

Direction all camera swing so focused upon face of operative me.

"This wretched human trash," host father say, "discarded by an uncaring socialist bureaucracy . . ."

This agent, watched under numerous camera, feel heat sensation rising blood glow within own cheek skin.

Continue host father, voice rising, say, "The nation that discarded this timid child, our weak, baffled guest, is a cruel country which persecutes free thinking and punishes ambition. A nation of crushing ideology." Say, "A dull, savage dictatorship reluctant to admit the faintest light of free speech or Christian charity . . ."

Among community member, citizen seated too dense, pressing shoulder, frequent face begin tilt forward, tilt back, repeat tilt to make head meaning agreement.

Vast cow father say, "It's from that tortured land of horror that this frightened child escaped—but for just six short months." Say, "This shivering, puny waif, this frail, vulnerable boy escaped the crushing misery of his government orphanage simply because a Christian missionary worked tirelessly to arrange six months of freedom and abundance for him and a ragtag assortment of his fellow orphans..."

Could be legs of operative me, muscle flex, spring above seated mob, repeat Lunging Lynx from Model United Nation, *swish-zonk*, decapitate population entire worship community. Lashing Lion, *rip-roar*, teeth of this agent eviscerate pack media scavengers.

Continued, endless host father say, "After months of negotiation, this emissary of Christian love shepherded her charges to the glorious shores of our blessed United States..." Say, "But for only a brief window of joy in a lifetime of bleakness and pain..."

Seated to one side, pig dog brother bend elbow so craft into sharp point, inject bony point to impact ribs of operative me, whisper say, "Check out Mom..."

Chicken host mother, head settle until sideways against own shoulder, eye iris contracted tiny dark pupil. Eye cover skins flutter, close, flash open. Drift close. Chicken mouth issue guttural snore.

Making huge inhales, host father say, "That suffering child came to live among us, to sing our songs and share the fellowship of our homes and church. He studied among our children, and they embraced and befriended him." Say, "This coarse, uneducated, illiterate boy came to excel at a recent spelling bee. He came to enjoy dancing American dances, and so popular did he become that he was chosen to represent our own United States of America at the Model United Nations..."

Seated opposite side this agent, cat sister keyboarding buttons atop surface personal telephone.

Remaining stance on altar, host father say, "Now, you might think an ignorant, backward child could never repay the generous gifts our community has granted him—the gifts of medical care, nutritious food, safe and secure shelter, free education, religious guidance and love—above all our love—but this child has repaid that debt."

Cow father cast eye so rest upon this agent. All entire eyeball of community rest on this agent.

Could be fists of operative me execute Punching Panda, *bam-blam*, so render entire crowd no conscious. Subsequent then execute Pumping Rabbit Maneuver distribute own seed among various appropriate vessel. Exit shrine. Seek midday nourishment. Visit memorial acclaimed war hero Colonel Sanders.

Host father say, "For it was this stooped, dirty waif who became the tool of sweet Jesus." Say, "It was through the wasted frame of this crippled, filthy orphan that Jesus Christ acted to stop an insane killer." Raising voice more loud, say, "Only by our Lord, controlling the puppet of this spindly, stunted wretch did justice advance on the demon which had taken possession of Trevor Stonefield." Shouting say, "It was that demon who cut short the lives of our children, but it was Christ who vanquished the demon before more damage could be inflicted."

Next now, voice stopped. Worship shrine silent. Awaiting.

Baking heat too many camera. Hearing expectation audio equipments.

Breaking silent, host father say, quiet to almost whisper say, "As the glorious agent of our savior, this beggar child has earned a permanent place in our community. A permanent place in our hearts." Voice rising, say, "And with that in mind, I propose that this boy remain among us, as a full and beloved member of the Cedar family."

Under eyes of camera, betrayed by satellite to global audience, eyes all world nation, cow father say, "I do hereby announce that it is my intention to fully and legally adopt the foreign exchange student our family calls Pygmy."

Faces total community, each fashioned as smile revealing all teeth. Wide smile compress cheek, obstruct eyes.

Hand raised open for testify, pledge, cow father say, "My wife and I do fully intend to become his guardians." Say, "Our son and daughter will become his siblings." Say, "And nothing—not international politics, nor diplomatic charges of kidnapping, nor bureaucratic red tape—will stand in our way. This dirty, sickly orphan, let us welcome him into the bosom of our fold. From this day forward, this puny, ignorant child will belong to us..."

For official record, witness here ever escalating semantics of ownership—operative me commenced in role exchange student sponsored of local religion. Charity program as organized by alive human cadaver Doris Lilly. Next becoming foster offspring. Next, acquired as adoption child. Ever increasing language American capitalism for ownership.

Esteemed Madam Fun Bags direct plump smile direction this agent, suggesting willing pubis. Suggest moist glisten excreted vaginal mucus. Welcoming engorged labium.

Only citizen no smile operative Tibor, operative Sheena, operative Magda.

No smile cadaver Zaire, East Timor, Egypt, or Brazil. Diet for arthropods.

From stance atop altar, surrounded multiple dead sacrifice

to violent United States culture of aggression, host father announce, say, "Yes, God has taken many of our brightest, stron-
gest, most beloved children, but God has given us a doomed,
discarded urchin that we, ourselves, can rescue . . ."

Same now, worship community explode with noise, every
citizens striking palms together making wild racket. All citizen wipe eyes of bleeding water, mopping waterlogged scraps
tissue. Hard exhaling so clear mucus out nostrils. Batter open
hands together. Next now advancing attack with open arms,
for ensnare with jagged finger, the flood citizen this community seeking trap this agent imprisoned under layers such
suffocating embrace, offer deadly passionate ardor.

Dispatch
Eighteenth

Begins here eighteenth account of operative me, agent number 67, recall most bad event occurring formative year ███████. Familial tragedy much documented history bureau ███████. Communicated to this agent via gentle wisdom top nurturing warden of district ███████. Occurrence tragedy dated back many year since infanthood this agent.

For official record, repeat recounting here early childhood history of operative me. For reinforce early important training of this agent.

Depicted here calendar date first-round academic testing to determine profession track each citizen four years beyond birth. Beginning of past today, this agent arise in residence shared among male and female parentage, two sibling sister, positioned concrete tower block multiple apartment among countless similar family unit. Out window of apartment able supervise gridlock vehicle traffic, supervise vista multitude concrete building roof, moistened apparel suspended for evaporate after laundry. Plentitude blouse, trouser, tunic fastened taut cordage, perform dance upon invisible wind music. Strut numerous pigeon.

Recall typical wait within hall passage, anxious stance among neighbor resident await to utilize shared toilet. So able forget bladder, male parentage prompting this agent: Multiply 12 to 3. List alphabet of *licorice*. Recite elements periodic table, so able hold water until toilet available.

During consume early meal, masticating stewed cereal

grains, voice of operative me muffled of crushed food, say, "...niobium, nitrogen, nobelium, osmium..."

Upon departure family apartment, en route small parade so arrive testing location, male parentage during command: Recite now man-made elements. Female parentage smoothing hair of operative me. Younger female siblings following behind. Voice of this agent say, "...rutherfordium, dubnium, seaborgium..." Male parentage demand: Recite now isotopes. Female parentage expectorate saliva so wet tissue to scrub at face of this agent. Along thoroughfare many such family, parentage accompany offspring bound today testing so determine future profession. To become architect or plumber or resource planner. All arriving institute of testing, stern facade no window, only guarded sentry flanking portal of towering doorway atop flight long slope many steep step.

Female parentage stoop until face level with face of operative me.

Male parentage offer hand for shake. Well wishes. Best luck.

Recall female parentage purse lips of face, offer gesture to contacts lips against face skin of this agent in expression so demonstrate affection.

However this agent decline. Too many peers present, too many possible witness such weak sentiment. Instead, offer hand for shake hand of female parentage.

Female fashion face of half smile. Accept hand.

Feet of operative me mount steps, climb slope amidst herd similar children compelled tested this day, dense flood such children, each alive since four years of birth. Child of future become physician. Become mechanical engineer. If poor tested, relegated refuse laborer. Compelled for mining salt. Mounting steps, trudge more high, children breathing whisper, "Igneous, metamorphic, sedimentary..." Weeping children pushed along with crowd. Other children whisper say, "Cumulus, stratus, cirrus..."

Adjacent child quotes relentless avatar, demented prophet Adolf Hitler, whisper say, "'He alone, who owns the youth, gains the future.'"

Arriving portal of building, stance high atop slope so many steps, eyes of operative me revolve head so look back, attempt regain vision parentage. No such fortunate. No able. From such far distant, all parentage massed together. No parentage distinct. At foot of slope steps, visible merely packed gray crowd. Motley ragged mob.

From below, must this agent also be lost amid similar crowd children.

Quote, "He alone, who owns the youth, gains the future."

Next now, this agent entering portal swept forward, buoyed by tide of shared generation. Washed through doorway routed with peers toward direction inevitable future, lips of operative me making quiet prayer of, "...radium, radon, rhenium, rhodium..." All swept down throat of hallway until portal heals behind, locked shut from past.

Dispatch
Nineteenth

Begins here nineteenth account of operative me, agent number 67, on arrival retail product distribution facility of city ▮▮▮▮▮. Outlet number ▮▮▮▮▮. Date ▮▮▮▮. For official record, no yet legal adopted so become full member host family Cedar. Making all effort resist absorption into American cult of the individual, traditional method entrenched oligarchy so maintain own power: Fracture citizen isolated into different religion, different race, different family. Label as rich culture diversity. Cleave as unique until each citizen stand alone. Until each vote invested no value. Single citizen celebrated as special—in actual, remaining no power.

Only when wedded to state purpose grants the citizen actual power. State mission and plan creates helpless individual as noble identity with grand reason for exist.

Arriving shopping mall, magic quiet door go sideways, disappear inside wall to open path from outside. Reveal inside stand old woman, Doris Lilly, slave woman appareled with red tunic, say, "Welcome to Wal-Mart." Say, "May I help you find something?"

Mouths of this agent make smile, face design into pleasing eye contact. This agent say, "Much venerate ancient mother ...to be commended such courage facing own imminent infirmity and demise..." Say, "Where sold here location 20 Mule Team Borax?" Say, "Available of purchase here cream of tartar?"

For official record, stationed sentry interior door Wal-Mart desiccated skeleton covered skin split infinite fissures, esteemed aged citizen cast eye on this agent, say, "Well, look at this..." Say, "If it isn't our little *hero.*"

Feet of operative me stance before lauded skeleton, this agent request assistance, ask location to acquire muriatic acid, additional obtain drain cleaner?

"Goodness," say top respected decayed cadaver, splay knurled fingers aligned either side knotted face, frame wide-circle eye and mouth so affected expression of surprise. Say, "Don't tell me you save the lives of innocent children *and* you do windows..."

Visible milling about interior Wal-Mart, operative Tibor, operative Mang. Additional visible top glorious Madam Party Pillows, lady delegate Malawi. Bodacious Madam Fun Bags, lady delegate Nepal.

Concealed interior trouser of operative me, paper American currency soiled fecal stain Trevor Stonefield, currency damp seed of this agent, partial saturated blood of clear-yellow bully.

"Cleaning supplies," say venerated dead-flesh mummy, "are on aisle fifteen."

Feet of operative me make small parade skirting labyrinth assembled packages printed many bright colors ink. Packages skinned tight glossy plastic. Plenteous plentitude too many objects ranked along shelf, bright faces begging for consumed before expiration. Best improved. Most strong taste. Dwindling worth mere days before rendered garbage by passing time.

In secret thinking machine of operative me recite quote violent cynic, socialist advocate Johann Most, within skull say, "Whoever looks at America will see: the ship is powered by stupidity, corruption, or prejudice."

Next then confronted enticing sweater meats, lady delegate Gambia. Caucasoid female boasting dolichocephalic-shape skull, one hand lifted so fingers entwined own brunette hairs, twist and stress hair tresses so demonstrate own superior health through strand tensile strength. Making displayed large eyes within receded zygomas, all indicate greater likelihood repeated numbers live offspring. Lady delegate fashion mouth to make facsimile engorged labium, say, "Hi." Say, "I didn't know you went here..."

Skull of operative me merely tilt forward to acknowledge. Stance paralyzed.

Within mind of operative me, in secret this agent say,... *gallium, germanium, gold...*

"Most times," say lady delegate Gambia, "I go to the Wal-Mart on Spring Vista Parkway, only sometimes I go to the Wal-Mart on Valley Drive." Stressing own hair, engorging facial labium, say, "Today I just decided to try a new Wal-Mart...and *here you are*!" Say, "Isn't that *weird*?"

Prowling within scope peripheral vision, operative Tibor observe scene. Encircle for surveillance. Tibor appareled typical American tunic, hem hang to knee level, black fabric printed alphabet English words "Mustache Rides 50 Cents."

Delegate Gambia say, "Thanks for saving my life the other day." Trail fingers of hand combing tresses. Trail fingers opposite hand so touching earlobe, dragged along line jawbone, trail down elegant tunnel of windpipe so arrive cleavage of mammary glands. Hand lingering at cleft, delegate say, "Maybe we could go out sometime?"

Additional prowling pig dog host brother, stance behind lady delegate, mocking with pig dog tongue extended, flickering pointed pink tip of own tongue muscle in direction delegate. Next, cupping own hands over own pectoral muscle to mimic glands, fingers twist and squeeze own invisible mammary glands.

Voice of operative me, issued most diplomatic tone, say, "Revered biggest madam..." Say, "Understood you already prior impregnated."

Hand stressing hair strand, fingers seize, paralyze. Lady Gambia say, "Huh?"

Head of operative me tilt toward direction distant operative Tibor. Neck muscle of that agent ringed purple hematomas, skin dented teeth bites. Tibor luggage basket contain baking soda, bleaching powder.

Eyes of lady delegate follow until cast on Tibor. Delegate say, "Oh, that." Say, "I skipped Algebra II yesterday, and went to Planned Parenthood." Finger of delegate lift from cleavage to fashion small flicker direction of Tibor.

Tibor fingers no flicker in return.

Feet of operative me continue parade so discover aisle fifteen, lye necessary for distill sodium hydroxide needed Operation Havoc. Tinner's fluid for obtain zinc chloride.

New now, approached by operative Metro for surrender to this agent vast wealth American dollar bills. Approached by operative Sheena, for granting this agent additional mass sum paper money secreted out religious food plates.

From growing distant, voice of lady delegate Gambia chase after this agent. Madam Gambia say, "Anytime you want." Away more far, more faint, voice say, "Maybe I'll see you at school?"

Next now, pig dog brother sidle adjacent stride of this agent. Marching in step, host brother say, "You're the man, Pygmy." Say, "From now on, you'll be up to your neck in hot, wet pussy."

Host brother describe how, this current now, authorities

conducting autopsy atop deceased decapitated corpse Trevor Stonefield. For explain aberrant behavior, butchering skull of clear-yellow hair, extracting brain for minute examine tumor. Hack fractured many pieces slaughtered bully. Mutilate into fragments pathetic corpse seeking possible answer. American ritual for render criminal harmless in death, remove blood, separate divide all vital organ. Total disassemble tainted flesh.

Host brother say, "Little man, you have *got* to learn me how to yank off folks' heads!"

Feet of operative me continue parade, secret recite, *Hafnium ...helium...holmium...*

Pig dog say, "I guess my sister is off-limits now that she's going to be your sister, too."

Within thinking machine of operative me, in secret this agent recite say,... *iridium, iron, iodine...*

Next now, approached by lavish chesticle lady delegate Haiti demonstrate standard mating behavior: waistband trouser lowered so reveal midriff, cleft of buttocks filled central strap pink-colored undergarment thong. Caucasoid female feature typical low degree of projection of alveolar ridge containing pristine teeth. Lady delegate separate glossy lips of face, say, "Hi, Pygmy..."

Feet of operative me continue parade.

Feet of pig dog brother cease, stance adjacent delegate Haiti, say, "Yo, hot mama." Say, "That's my new kid brother you're hitting on."

For official record, no brother. No yet adopted. No official. Perhaps no never.

Continued along parade, this agent respond over own shoulder, say, "Most honored lady..." Continue parade, say, "Are you no already vessel for reproductive seed of Mang?"

From behind, fading in distant, lady delegate say, "It's okay. I went to the school nurse..." Receding more faint, say, "I got those morning-after plan B pills..."

Within mind of operative me, in secret this agent keep say,... *tin, titanium, tungsten...*

Pig dog brother, lady delegate Haiti, both remain abandoned in trail of operative me.

Small parade arrive aisle fifteen, wall of packages stacked mothballs for extracting napthalene. Vast array bottle milk of magnesia to yield magnesium hydroxide. Infinite selection alum for aluminum sulfate. Ammonia combined water for ammonium hydroxide. Carbolic acid for phenol. Borax for distill sodium borate. Ingredients massed necessary all component of science fair project.

Execution Operation Havoc. Massive debacle.

Next now, voice say, female voice say from behind, "Congratulations, comrade." Revealed as voice operative Magda, at helm large basket crafted silver wire, roll atop wheels. Magda commence select chrome alum, deposit interior basket, say, "You demonstrate superior mental brilliance."

Magda continue select vinegar, effective source ingredient acetic acid, place bottle vinegar within wheel basket, say, "You rescue a handful ridiculous, silly American children..." Say, "So soon we may kill millions..."

Quote, "Whoever looks at America will see: the ship is powered by stupidity, corruption, or prejudice."

Tibor approach, limb arm hoisting basket munitions, baking soda, corn syrup, chlorine bleach. Drill focus glower eye upon face skin this agent, Tibor say, "Such crafty agent to deserve much lauded." Fashion Tibor hand shape Beretta semiautomatic, index finger as thirty-five-millimeter barrel. Comrade aim flesh weapon direction skull sutures operative me.

Say Tibor, "Comrade, perhaps best revisit mental narrative operative Pavel." Say, "Always most-bright fire first to be extinguish." Same now, Tibor discharge pretend pistol, eject fictitious bullet so feign expunge gray meatloaf this agent.

Pantomime so suggest operative me how easily erased.

Dispatch
Twentieth

Begins here twentieth account of operative me, agent number 67, most recent exited public mass transportation routed ███████. Deposited industrial park ███████. Made lengthy parade so arrive private facility performing research contracted United States federal department of ███████. Specific purpose to abscond taking top security samples ███████.

For official record, during conveyance aboard public vehicle, simultaneous host cat sister apply paint color black upon face skin of operative me, this agent espousing profound truths presented revered French demographer Alfred Sauvy, make sermon how modern world struggle between corrupt degenerate menace of capitalism and the noble socialist, battling for control or rescue of the innocent third world. Voice of operative me, bold voice trumpeting so inform all proletariat within vehicle, proclaim former slave colonies third world prospective victim capitalist hungry greed over raw natural resources, stealing petroleum, raping of mineral bauxite and zinc, in return dumping on innocents only inferior products decadent mass culture. Wily capitalists flooding native economies too many destructive corrosives—refined sugar, of example, Hollywood movie star, heated seat automobile, SPAM, paste of teeth, tissue of toilet, Bionic Man, permanent wave.

Ear of cat sister tuned attentive, host sister apply finger rubbing black paint about face skin of this agent, sister accept political truths declared Sauvy in 1952. Top celebrated missive titled "Three Worlds, One Planet."

Weapon of operative me, constrained turgid within trouser this agent.

Heralding voice of operative me, loudly vociferate how all wealthy nations innate evil. Converse, all poverty nations innocent and source much oppressed goodness. Cite additional vast brilliant Brandt Report dated 1980 proofed beyond facts how greedy oil-consuming giants of North Hemisphere—specific Canada, United States, Britain, and Australia—starved starving South Hemisphere nations of Zambia, Soviet Union, and Saudi Arabia. Shrill cry of operative me expanding more loud, more until voice break, become shriek, this agent say, "The fuel such low expensive able propel this public vehicle..." Say, "Petroleum, in actual poverty blood sucked out aboriginal child."

Manifesto presented so bold.

Chin jawbone of this agent tilted high in courage defiant. Await agreement.

Cat sister smooth paint upon stilled lips of operative me. Skin of this agent stiff from dry paint. Stroke smooth, massage. Gentle circle. Greased finger lick infinite tiny licks. Slippery sister finger slide width of this agent heated forehead.

Succulent fragrant bosom so nearby. Host sister touching with fingertip, say, "You know, you have the prettiest eyes..."

Head of operative me, neck rotate so able visible own eyeballs reflection upon interior night window. Window of public vehicle reveal merely this agent, blotted black, eye sunk deep within black paint.

Host sister fingertipping lip of this agent, cat sister say, "It's too bad you're going to be my brother..."

Seated captain of public conveyance halt vehicle, activate

door so becomes unhealed in metal wall, decree through amplified microphone, say, "End of the line." Say, "All *mimes* please disembark."

During host sister and this agent exit conveyance, vehicle captain offer hand containing ink pen. Offer hand clenched tablet blank paper pages. Say, "You're the kid who killed that crazy motherfucker." Captain say, "Do you mind if I get your autograph?"

Traversing dark environment en route destination, surrounded mating cry cricket, croak of bulls frog, lecture this agent concerning France missive entitled *Le Defi Americain*. How admonish intellectual elite over manner United States numerous multinational corporation Kodak, Gillette, General Motor endeavor tangle entire globe ensnared tentacles sucking wealth for digest and fatten parent sovereign American nation, leeching life energy addition opportunity during render subject nation stripped resources and native cultures.

Current now doing pilgrimage perimeter industry park, bordered fence linked chain. Navigate thick darkness. Tread macadam roadway empty of vehicle, approach distant building constructed clay brick, washed under illumination large electric bulb perched atop multiple pole. Macadam field painted branched white alignment fitting infinite automobile lazy American bourgeois professional. Current now, stored no automobile.

Railing voice of operative me continue announce guilt portion deserved heaped upon Western nations according enlightened saga Pearson Report issued United Nations Conference on Trade and Development—

"Hush," say prowling cat sister. Say, "Just *shush* for a minute, okay?"

Sister halted, hands extended, fingers spread feeling blackness, sensing chilled wind for sound sentry guards. Possible witness recording document via video camera.

"You're the *trainee* spy," say host sister, shaking straight finger at face of this agent. Sister touch finger to shut lips of operative me, say, "I need you to keep quiet."

Regardless pressure for instruct sole correct political ideology.

Regardless continued fallacy engaging worldview host sister.

In secret, within head, this agent reciting, *Americium . . . antimony . . . argon . . .*

Crouched posture lower primate, sprint sawtooth pattern so bisect mowed landscape largest building. Arriving sign stationed at entry lettered in English words to read: RADIO-LOGICAL INSTITUTE OF MEDICINE.

Often possible conquest cat sister, sling no conscious atop mowed landscape, gift with fetus bearing same pretty eyes as operative me.

Next now arrive doors of facility, sister sling fabric sack, dive hand inside so retrieve laminated name card of host father, prosthetic human eye crafted green color glass. Cat sister dash card against box adjacent doors. Position eye at focus of box lens. Same current now, door of building, latch sound clack, angry humming. Host sister hand grasp edge released door swing so unhealed in wall stacked red-color bricks.

Voice of operative me beseech no abandon, no relegate duty mere lookout. Bid this agent accompany sister along foray for harvest resources to equip science fair project.

This agent projecting voice beg mercy, words compressed down to fast rush reedy breath delivered out constriction throat. Peaked muscle of face, forehead stiff of flaking black color paint, yawning both eye wide around and skinned glistening water. Windpipe of operative me make swallow, jump apple of Adam gulp sound. Brimming eye similar baby puppy American eat as beef.

Host sister observe delicious face expression this agent. Sister narrow eye, cast glance so whisk surround landscape, say, "Okay." Inject hand within fabric sack, extract skins of latex for fit stretched over fingers. Deliver latex skin to this agent, during say, "Just wear these so you don't leave a bunch of fingerprints."

Latch door remain angry hum. Impatient to be returned so healed in wall.

Sister stretch each own hands within similar latex skins. Usher this agent so violate portal. Allow door heal, humming cease.

That now, victory of operative me encroach extreme top secret facility United State defense contractor. Surrounded lavish decadent luxury of military industrial complex. Infinite computer screen boast four-color display. Fountains dispensing chilled waters to swallow. Spa title MEN. Plethora chair atop wheels, balanced so pivot in all direction. Floor layered rich gray carpet. Lavish luxury playground deeded use of evil engineer, wicked biochemist.

Already cat sister making parade, leading this agent along labyrinth many fences upholstered elegant gray canvas, zigzagging so avoid missteps en route destination. Each writing desk allowed luxury of private fenced territory. Fastened canvas fence surface selection photographs depicting obese American infants wallowing atop arms obese parentage, smothered amid needless vast inventory playthings. Photographs of animal, dog and cat, beef and pork. Occasional soiled vessel crafted dense ceramic, residue dried caffeine, glazed with legend "World's Greatest Dad."

Arriving cabinet, doors of tall cabinet painted gray metal, host sister deliver fabric sack to this agent. Instruct for hands of operative me position opening of sack stretched wide. Host sister grasp cabinet handle, say, "The best *loot* is in here..."

Hand twist handle. Swing metal door so unhealed. Reveal interior of cabinet small packages crafted pulp paper, light cardboard. Sister commence violate each package, discover contents, and dispense into waiting fabric sack.

Perhaps mistake.

During harvest contents cabinet, sister say, "Did you hear the autopsy results on Trevor Stonefield?" Say, "My dad heard from some medical guy at the county." Say, "Turns out, somebody was molesting him—Trevor, I mean, not the county guy..."

Certainly mistake. Collecting within fabric sack, merely color spectrum many ink pens. Harvesting small packages chrome wire bent so clip papers. Ammunition American staplers. Scissor. Additional ink pen.

Cat sister continue speech concerning Trevor autopsy, how discover recent trauma large intestine. Abrasions partially healed of rectum. Faded hematoma. Fissures torn tender membranes Trevor anus. All indicators past recent sexual abused.

Same as water bin chew white rodent. Same as Pavel. The deity models only correct behavior, killing by cancer warfare, by earthquake and cyclone. All human must justify future vicious murder by the deity.

Host sister ladling into fabric sack packages blank computer disk. Adhesive label. Tablets graph papers. Mechanical pencil. Gum eraser.

Same now, available nearby such selection nuclear missile launch codes. Tantalizing details strategic American troop movements. Plans preliminary prototype future most scientific military weapons. Abundant cornucopia every top defense secret.

Host sister, purloining more ink pen, more graph paper, say, "The police are *totally* going to bust somebody for buttfucking Trevor..."

Here particular installation stockpiled delicious nuclear isotopes. Plutonium. Strontium. Delectable menu radioactive elements. In secret, reciting this agent, *Uranium...radium ...einsteinium...* Wide selection deadly chemical, biological culture sample.

Anthrax. Ebola. Sarin.

For access, merely utilize laminate name card, green color prosthetic eye. Both secreted trouser cat sister.

Thin fabric sack stretched almost to failure, filled burden ink pens, staplers, adhesive tapes, blank disk, debris. Detritus.

Making voice of baby puppy, this agent beseech sister retreat, attain location storage of nuclear materials so private enough able exchange mouths. Saliva commingle. Regress to vault top security for generate mutual pleasure. There access smorgasbord curium, hassium, lawrencium.

Cat sister heal doors of cabinet, close handle. Turn to cast eyes upon this agent, say, "Pygmy..." Say, "Get this—you and me are going to have the same dad, so we can't make out, and we can't get him in trouble." Say, "You got that?"

In secret voice operative me, within head quote jolly monarch, good-natured king Mao Tse-tung, say, "The need to shit after eating does not mean that eating is a waste of time."

Hands of operative me encased latex, burdened anchor weight stolen pens, postage stamps. In secret, this agent say within head, debate will police arrest for sodomy clear-yellow bully. Abort deadly science fair project. Foil Operation Havoc.

Punish for sodomy by place operative me imprisoned full lifetime accompanied numerous sodomites. Such the absurdity American legal justice.

Awaiting nearby, enticing radioactive isotope polonium-210, iridium-192, cesium-137. So almost attainable, poisoned treasure of exquisite thallium. So close within reach fragrant bosom cat sister, lavish enriched thorium. Combination all glorious victory.

Quote, "The need to shit after eating does not mean that eating is a waste of time."

Only already now, prominent buttock cat sister in retreat. Regressing away, say, "I can't tell folks how to act in *your* town, but here..." Say, "Brothers and sisters just do *not* get busy with each other." Trouser fabric stretched so conceal succulent host sister buttock, making rapid stealth parade toward direction sign of exit.

Dispatch
Twenty-first

Begins here twenty-first account of operative me, agent number 67, on revisit religion propaganda distribution outlet of city ██████. Exterior worship shrine menaced simmering horde media jackal for printed journal ██████. In attendance, multiple parasite representing crowded whorehouse of cable distributed television outlet ██████. Additional under siege by loitering vultures radio network ██████.

For official record, today occasion purposed discarding mortal remains Trevor Stonefield. Ritual display of Trevor corpse prior feed for nourishment arthropods, bacterium, and microbe.

Combining melee media jackals, roadway occupied busy cavalcade citizens, pacing blockage entrance of shrine. Raising forest of cardboards mounted wooden post for handle, cardboard printed English letter words, KILLERS DON'T DESERVE SALVATION. Other signage written, NO TEARS FOR TREVOR. Righteous chaos wagging cardboard, chanting, repeat chant, "Trevor Stonefield burns in hell..." Citizen mothers, citizen fathers, and offspring, making small parade describing continuous ellipse before shrine, chanting, "Trevor Stonefield burns in hell..."

Styled female hyena painted claw clutch microphone emblazed large Arabic numeral four, hyena make stance at immediate focus camera lens. Appareled uniform business suit, face painted so erase all defect, female hyena cast gaze within camera, say, "Even today as grieving, angry families protest outside the funeral of the troubled young man, the county medical examiner continues to investigate recent autopsy findings..." Say, "Forensic evidence which proves the school shooter, himself, was the victim of a recent violent sexual assault."

Female hyena cease issue proclamation, fashions mouth to make smile, say, "Did my hair look okay?" Hand hook flat item out own trouser, manipulate so item cleaves to produce small mirror. Eyeing own visage, media hyena say, "Does my eye shadow look balanced?"

Frenzied journalist attracted stench of human tragedy. Horde scavenger feast at overflowing anus of world history.

Skirting perimeter carnival, disorder jumble negative emotion, stealth limbs operative me gain access worship shrine. Enter perpetual twilight common all worship shrine. Dim interior, absent burning cylinder paraffin, absent fragrant garish display genitals of plant life. Minus congregants. No corroded mummy Mrs. Lilly. Merely casket cleaved so display cadaver buoyed aloft upholstery blue fabric silk, below plaster feet fake dead man bleeding red paint. Corpse eye cover skins healed shut. Trevor Stonefield. Reclined appareled blouse appropriate normal worship occasion, neck bound silk knotted banner. Curtain clear-yellow hair frame Trevor face atop head cushion. Grid bruised of tile grout, faint red lines behind corpse face powder.

Stance positioned behind casket, male issue endless stream English word. Devil Tony. Babble litany gibberish eternal life everlasting...innocent...no blame...

Seated most-forward bench of audience, male and female. Parentage Trevor Stonefield. Appareled entirely black color. Respective faces leaking mucus into disposable paper tissues.

Female face shrouded underneath black color fishnetting suspended from same-color head cover.

Infiltrating from roadway, chant voices. Shout repeating, "Trevor Stonefield burns in hell... Trevor Stonefield burns in hell..."

Within shrine, timid voice devil Tony, hoarse resulting damaged during attack operative Magda. Submucosal throat hemorrhage. Overwhelmed raucous noise chanting rabble. Droning devil Tony continue denouncing clear-yellow bully as deranged, insane lunatic. Deriding Trevor as occupied by demon from Western-concept Satan. Spinning excuse for hope deity accept and tolerate pathos dead adolescent.

In secret, voice of operative me say within head, quote benevolent emperor, jovial helmsman Benito Mussolini, say, "The history of saints is mainly the history of insane people."

Every men must earn future torture, cruel extinction allotted of the deity. Even during man stance upon knee, jabber prayer into folded hand, behave having most benevolent kindness, even during such good acts—the deity already seed cancer into prostate, already dispatch lunatic so murder offspring of man most beloved. The deity craves sin of man as justify monstrous pain of fate the deity enjoys inflict.

Guilt of man assuages guilt of the deity. Human cruelty enable greater cruel practice of the deity.

At siege exterior shrine, chanting anger, "... Trevor Stonefield burns in hell..."

Contained interior, crushing shame clear-yellow bully parentage. Devil Tony beseeching mercy for Western God accept damaged, imperfect mortal residue.

Feet of operative me take stance at rear of worship shrine, balanced point between anger and shame. Secret recite within skull this agent, no voice say,...*actinium, aluminum, americium*...

In actual, the deity probable much welcome spirit slain bully. The deity prefer citizen execute mistake. So gain educated as benefit incorrect actions. Best evidence rich living experience, most full fulfill attempt potential lingering sense regret. Regret top reward. Regret most-sweet accomplishment—best prove citizen utilize opportunity, attempt forever growth and continuous develop.

Folded, concealed within trouser of operative me, bundle paper American currency stained fecal, blood of Trevor. Smudged seed of this agent. Dwindling monetary unit remain beyond forced violent sodomy. Hand of this agent extract soiled currency, conceal wrapped within fist.

Next now, voice droning devil Tony, jabber halt. Shrine filled waiting, shadowed faint din, "...burns in hell..." Face devil Tony tilt back so cast eye on this agent.

Quote, "The history of saints is mainly the history of insane people."

Eye of devil Tony await, prompt parentage Stonefield revolve heads for witness this agent. Faces male and female parentage, crushed with fissures, crumpled canyons flesh channel water bleeding out eyes, face skin purple-red with blood glow.

Filth dollars tight inside fist of operative me. Retaining stance made rear of shrine.

Male parentage lift self, knees made straight until attain standing posture. Eyes remain cast upon this agent, male parentage face luminous layered water, male lift own hand, scoop air so suggest agent advance. Approach casket, deceased cadaver, devil Tony.

Trevor nose formerly folded sideways, restored so straight forward. Electric-bolt-blue-color eye, forever asleep. Curtain yellow hair furrowed with many combing. Hairs pruned for to meet top deity.

Thinking machine operative me ponder. Gray meatloaf ensconced skull of this agent weigh ethics, obligation for make confess. Possible resolve much emotion, confusion, mental turmoil suffering Stonefield parentage. Possible explain savage anal assault astride men spa. Confession affection expressed Trevor bully, attributed Stockholm syndrome. Explain every factors causative infamous outburst upon Model United Nation.

Next then, possible to forfeit this agent affection esteemed cat sister.

Possible scuttle noble mission Operation Havoc.

Squander adoration Team Family Cedar.

Negate admiration all fellow citizen immediate community.

Recite secret within skull of operative me, say no voice, ...*antimony, argon, arsenic*...

Next now, feet of operative me take initial stride forward, direction mourning and death.

Dispatch
Twenty-second

Begins here twenty-second account of operative me, agent number 67, recall most bad event occurring formative year ▇▇▇▇▇▇. Occurrence familial tragedy related terrorist assassination dated ▇▇▇▇▇▇. Massacre innocent citizens municipal area ▇▇▇▇▇.

For official record, repeat recounting here early childhood history. For reinforce early important training of this agent. Bottom worst trauma shaping life of operative me.

Depicted here scene conducting first-round academic testing to determine profession track each young citizen. All student present dated four years beyond birth. Seated infinite row metal desk, sequestered interior Ministry of Future Building subsequent departing company of parentage at entry portal. Male and female parentage this agent last witnessed remaining below foot steep slope entrance step. Making ascent series tall step, each step more height than knee joint this agent, each leg of operative me required raise almost so knee impact chest so gain conquest level next step. Horde entire generation such children scaling slope, struggle accomplish each step, until eventual revolve heads so discover all parentage reduce to rabble, no face distinct.

Next then, ushered all child navigating passageways more deep within building, directed always turn right, turn left, wait. Directed no speaking. No remove overcoats.

In secret this agent reciting, no voice within skull say, *Nobelium, osmium, oxygen* . . .

Echoing footsteps children arrive cavern no windows, lined rows of desk infinite as wave after wave between ocean beach and horizon. Vast interior acreage such countless metal desk. Instructed each young assume seated. No speak. Instructed await additional orders.

Desk of operative me, surface defaced, gouged former occupant, Arabic numbers years receding before parentage this agent. Gouged so record years prior glorious, revered ancestors. So prevalent vandalism, document tedium of past children awaiting test. Frustrate from idle. Anxious of dread future career today will determine—physician versus excavator of corpse hole. Benighted civil engineer versus lowly scrubber of floor.

Carved scarred into surface desk, scratched deep, words quote learned minister, noble general Adolf Hitler, writing say, "The victor will never be asked if he told the truth."

Additional probable state in secret observe during children await test. Probable numerous concealed camera. Listing note whether child obey orders, seated patient demonstrating no anxious. Fold hands, eye directed ahead. Or other: whether make child trouble, fidget, suited only career butchering offal.

Beyond many long now, slow now, lingering now, squad many monitor make entrance. Make long parade along every row desk, distribute paper test, many sheet. Apportion each child single pointed pencil. Monitors instruct: as child complete test, to rise. Exit vast hall through door entered. Relinquish complete test to exit monitor.

Career test request such typical information: define De Moivre's Theorem. Apply equation of angular momentum. Calculate area utilizing polyhedron formula. Demonstrate Avrami equation. Biot-Fourier equation. Rotational kinetic energy equation. List atomic weight manganese. Latitude longitude city Reykjavik. Nothing asked beyond intellect of most idiot child. Simple task. Require no effort. Limited solely facile knowledge.

Translate Celsius into Fahrenheit. Translate foot-pounds into Newton meters.

Utilize Feuerbach's Theorem. Sylow's Theorem.

Questions no justify such concern. Date signed Treaty of Ghent. Distance between Earth and moon, Earth and Mars, Mars and Jupiter.

Thinking machine of operative me make hasty completed of test, write accurate response all question. Make stance, and deliver test to monitor. Next now, directed follow new monitor along passageway. Almost all majority fellow children remain seated, scratching own heads, biting own teeth marks deep into wood pencil shaft, head tilted low above own paper. Other children, skulls nested atop desk of folded arms, asleep.

Joyous, this agent make rapid parade so reunion parentage, announce how simple test, announce answer every correct so probable become physician, engineer, prominent chemist. Future such prestige, able provide parentage secure role status. Perhaps allotted own private toilet. Perhaps rationed private automobile. So joyous, this agent no noted course directed so arrive new, more-small chamber. Repeat instructed assume seat, this desk among merely handful fellow children. Later discover children names Magda, Oleg, Ling, Tibor. All among room born since four year ago, Mang, Pavel, Boban, Sheena, and Bokara. Present Vaky, Metro, Sasha, Chernok, Tanek, Vigor, all future peer of operative me.

For official record, all youth no speak, maintain seated, hand folded, head erect.

Later discover, all present children score perfect in career test.

Door of room remaining healed in wall.

In secret reciting this agent, tiny prayer, within head say no voice, *Samarium, scandium, selenium*...So eager repeat witness plentitude laundry, blouse, trouser, tunic perform dance upon invisible wind music. Observe strut numerous pigeon.

However, next then door no healed, swing so display state officer uniformed executive guard, heart of tunic plated thick layer many gold medals, many ribbons red color. Belted with sidearm Beretta nine-millimeter, semiautomatic pistol. Penetrate room shod two boot black polish leather. Advance boot until attain stance before present young.

Executive guard remove uniform head cover, wedge between own elbow and torso, at parade rest cast eyes so contacted each child present, guard say, "Congratulations." Guard delve own hand deep within uniform trouser so extract square folded paper. Make no folded. White paper printed words. Guard position paper so obscure own eyes, next then begin read, say, "'Proved here the top promising citizens from next glorious generation our state.'"

Executive guard acclaim how majority fellow students continue struggle completing test. As such, offer limited talents for the future state. At top best, perhaps to become mere nuclear physicist or aerospace engineer.

"'However,'" say executive guard, continue read out paper, "'among children of this room, will control of future entire state become deeded. Granted those present full authority pinnacle positions state and party.'"

Next then express great sorrow for to deliver additional dour message. Reminds executive guard, enormous fact how American nation constant first enemy our peaceful gracious civilization. Corrupt, degenerate America. Guard reiterates statistics recent past history United State terrorist attacks targeting our innocent citizens. Cites frequent recent American suicide bombers. Corrosive Hollywood movie.

"'As our top potential leaders,'" read, say executive guard off paper, "'you must open your skull to the esteemed wisdom offered Lenin, Mao, Perón.'" Guard voice gaining more loud, say, "'Must you hollow your skull for welcome the revered guidance by Hitler, Stalin, and Trotsky.'"

From morning of today, all present become adopted offspring of the state. Government will raise for glorious adulthood.

"Beyond today," say executive guard, "you will never again be alone in your mind."

All future thoughts, so become mere echoes state teaching. Enlightened ideological education.

During morning of today, guard read aloud out paper, suffered center of capital city most massive attack American terrorist to date. Simultaneous time of career testing, enemy agents sourced the United States detonated dirty nuclear device, murdering countless, contaminating wide sector. Parentage of all present reported casualty. Slaughtered at whim American demons. Most beloved familial relations butchered screaming by United States covert military actions.

Executive guard lower paper printed words, resume folded, secrete deep within trouser pocket. Guard say, "By no mourning—only diligent study—requested children of the state best honor martyred ancestors." Say, "In repeat, congratulations on such successful testing."

Quote, "The victor will never be asked if he told the truth."

Recalling this agent how recently rejected lips of female

parentage, fearing ridicule from peer. How instead merely grasp hand.

Executive guard replace uniform head cover upon skull, say, "Of top important, must state now plot revenge upon American devils." Say, "Follow me." Guard pivot so exit room, leading Tibor, Chernok, Vaky, Magda...all operative taking first strides into next future family. Follow exact stride of executive guard, forward march standard 22.5 inch, every eight stride traveling five yard more deep into new mission deadly vengeance.

Dispatch
Twenty-third

Begins here twenty-third account of operative me, agent number 67, attending compulsory education session public institution ▮▮▮▮▮. Class period ▮▮▮▮▮. Physical education conducted instructor Coach ▮▮▮▮▮. For official record, American education rituals especial efficient at task segregation youth of superior intellect removed from youth gifted superior physical prowess. Best example, ritual label as "dodgeball." Therein all peer males engage mock battle under witness fertile peer females.

Commencement of ritual, physical superior males select best combatants for accompany into battle, thus ranking all from most-best to least desirable for reproduction during females note close attention. Next then, divided males engage violent assault upon each opposite army, battering with inflated bladders latex rubber.

Over course conflict, males boasting superior musculature inflict injure upon males typical of superior intellect although suffering inferior height-to-weight ratio, body mass index, and stature.

At completion dodgeball ritual, females made full aware which males present most-desirable physical traits. Vanquished males culled by injury, weak reproductive citizens force self-select, redirect, instead impregnate mates, procreate offspring, instead channel aggressions chess club, focus sexual ambitions science club. Debate or forensics. Model rocket association. Granted no access sexual reproduction, thereby liberate superior intellect for indulge in further education. During same, superior physical genetics routed so impregnate superior physical females.

For benefit all society, most crucial segregate intellect out physical fit.

All accomplished in battle dodge of ball.

For official record, prior this today operative me forever selected final for dodgeball army. Captains respective armies bicker over negotiate inclusion this agent. Captain say, "We'll take the gimp and the retard if you take Pygmy..."

Forever during, peer group females observe, issue exaggerate facial features express disgust, pinch nostrils shut, protrude tongue muscles, making straight finger at direction this agent.

Except this today, no occur such scenario.

This today, most large majority fellow male student appareled fabric tunic, black fabric printed English alphabet words "Property of Jesus." Recounting accurate, this agent. Such many peer males appareled identical tunic of operative me. Male student arrive arena gymnasium, approach this agent, say, "Yo, Pygmy, my man." Say, "You'll be on my team, right?"

Peer males assemble so reproductive females observe from distance opposite portion arena gymnasium. Among males, exceptions no appareled black tunic operative me, no approach this agent, only operative Tibor, Oleg, Chernok. All fellow operatives, chosen long-ago today of career testing, created orphan American terrorist that dismal passed today, operatives Ling, Mang, Tanek, merely stand in distant. Cast pointed eye upon this agent.

During same now, former male delegate Brunei demand,

say, "Pygmy, show me that thing where you break people's legs."

Other delegate, Burundi, say, "No, first teach us how to knock everybody out with your elbow..."

Crowding each aside, gentleman delegate Laos say, "Pygmy, little dude, show us how to kill guys with just your pinkie finger."

Ballooning chest with vast inhale, voice of operative me quote benign dictator, ambitious regent Idi Amin, say, "'Politics is like boxing—you try to knock out your opponents.'"

Next now, door comes unhealed from wall of gymnasium, door swings to display instructor for period of dodgeball.

Moment American instructor display self in door, students all stand and say, all unison one voice, "Greetings, esteemed most revered educator. Accept, please, our gratitude for the wisdom you impart."

All American youth, male and female, say such.

Sole exception this agent.

Immediate all student bidding for this agent warrior among team, beseeching accompany into battle of inflated latex bladders. Forced settle dispute using traditional ritual hurtling monetary coin at roof, allow final position of tumbling coin to decide: head or tails. In capitalist nation, all is decided by money. Beyond this agent, each army assembled conscripting best physical specimen. Armies take position opposite walls gymnasium. Provisioned equal quantity inflated bladder.

Instructor physical education insert metal snail, silver-color snail, between own face lips. Instructor exhale snail so create shrill sound whistle, same now bladders fly.

Space gymnasium echoing impact rubber bladders. Bounce

and slam contact with basketball wood of floors. Slap hit of impact rubber skidding, abrading human skin. Squeal lining of athletic shoe barking against floor varnish. Thunder of running feet, chased feet, charging shoes. Bladder hurtle such speed trailing scream before skinning cheek skin of president chess club. Welting shoulder, swollen red welt, National Merit Scholar.

Amid volley such deadly bladders, former gentleman delegate Bahrain say, "Little dude, teach me that backward kick..."

Requests instruction Exploding Mule *kick-sock*.

Former delegate Myanmar pitch bladder so protect this agent, say, "Hey, Pygmy... show me the other kicking deal."

Requests instruction Flying Hyena *lash-pow*.

Amid skirmish, landing hail infinite stinging bladders, rampant battlefield speeding missile, operative Tanek take position near elbow this agent. Tanek say whisper, keyed low so audible only ear of operative me, say, "Attention, comrade." Say, "Become no seduced by silly adoration of American devils."

Next then, unseen bladder smite face cheek of operative Tanek. Rules of engagement require that agent extract self out battle, retire to margin gymnasium.

Eyes all fellow operative condemn this agent.

Hands of operative me procure inflated bladder. Arms catapult bladder so impact opposing team soldier, operative Otto, deemed among best top army of school. Render Otto fallen, clutching rib cage writhing prone on basketball wood, Otto eyes biting tight shut, bleeding water. Army of operative me issuing massive cheer. All fellow soldier impacting open hands on scapular of this agent. Peer fingers disarray head hairs of operative me. Say, "Way to go, Pyg-ster."

Quick then, seize new bladder, hurtle so smite operative Bokara, impacting so sternum that agent issue *crack* sound. Operative Bokara embrace own self, topple until supine.

Witnessing females cheer. Stance among crowd females, operative Magda observe with sorrow eye, hands of that agent stroking own flat abdomen. Mammary glands swollen new hormone flood.

Under death stare fellow operatives, this agent intercept flight speeding bladder, grasp and rocket so stun forehead operative Ling. Impact bladder erupt vast wealth of viscous red blood, explode out nose of that agent. Bladder bounce aside, stamping print blood, print blood, print blood across basketball wood.

Host pig brother trumpet breath to say, "That's my brother!" Trumpet, "Smear those *foreigners!*"

Operative Ling removed from battlefield. Skirmish continued. Dodging munitions numerous stinging bladders, feet of operative me take stance adjacent pig dog brother. Under heavy fire, say, "Respected brother . . ." Say, dodging incoming bladder, say, "Procure eight count of Rohypnol pills of sleep, and will train you Punching Panda." Say, "Make of brother top best invincible."

Next then, flying grab hands of this agent, intercept bladder for rescue other fellow soldier, former delegate Congo. To gentleman delegate say, "Acquire one container fabricated steel metal, capacity two cubic feet for purpose science fair . . ." Say, "In return, promise teach Striking Cobra Quick Kill maneuver."

Hurtling bladder so assassinate opposing soldiers, clutter battlefield many casualty, this agent bargain will teach Soaring Condor Double Strike to first man who deliver five pounds potassium nitrate fertilizer. Will instruct Leaping Kangaroo

Punch Escape to man able provide blasting cap. Will coach Lunging Lynx beheading yank to anyone granting battery-operated timing device.

Against backdrop frequent casualty, bombarding heavy artillery rubber bladders, this agent assign former gentleman delegate Equatorial Guinea, precipitate nitrogen tri-iodide sourced ammonium hydroxide of school laboratory. Assign former delegate Mali distill reagent flowers of sulfur. Amidst carnage of battle, assign delegate Peru source 17.67 ounce most purified sodium peroxide.

Forever continues flurry of war. Brave action noble soldiers engaged in practice of dying. Youth enrolled, greedy to learn killing. Squeal soles so many shoe. Thud impact velocity bladders. Famished for violence.

Next now, former gentleman delegate Mozambique say, "Pygmy, my man." Offer elbow bent own arm, say, "Now break my arm!" Say, "I got a test on *Silas Marner* next period."

Request of delegate timing device.

Mozambique say, "Would my clock radio work...?"

Same now, fists of operative me hammer *bam-blam*, Giant Stork Death Kick, snapping puny ulna delegate, compound fracturing so bone emerge out ruptured skin of youth fore-arm. Upon sound, bone crack, pop out muscle tissue, at now when Mozambique witness, delegate soldier roll own eyeballs backward in skull. Skeleton buckle at knees, buckle at waist and neck. Collapse upon basketball wood. No conscious. No *Silas Marner.*

Quote, "Politics is like boxing—you try to knock out your opponents."

Revered instructor breathing shrill noise out silver snail. Travels inflated bladder imprinting spilled nose blood out

Ling, bounce blood onto wood, onto face soldiers smeared red, warrior hands stained blood.

Location dodgeball war—same location of ritual mating dance. Same location as Model United Nations. Chipped in concrete wall, ricochet bullet out pistol of Trevor Stonefield. From perimeter this gymnasium, casualty Tibor, casualty Otto and Bokara and Ling, cast eye pledging patient future attack upon this agent.

Next now, numerous fellow soldier: former delegates Antigua, Latvia, Lesotho, delegates Nauru, Namibia, Nigeria, all learning nothing of *Silas Marner*, dreading test, all take stance so fists of operative me may *bam-blam* quick render them helpless cripple.

Dispatch
Twenty-fourth

Begins here twenty-fourth account operative me, agent number 67, seated surrounding meal table host family Cedar. American holiday food of Thanksgiving. Present: vast cow father, pig dog brother, chicken mother, cat sister host family all hands linked so create fence surrounding bounty food table. Recite religious incantation ███████. Express gratitude such bounty slaughtered enemy citizens of ███████. Nation boast celebration vanquish aboriginal North American peoples ███████.

For official record, intestines of operative me infinite sickened gorging diet typical United State household. Cooked muscle tissues of Colonel Sanders. So infinite such array various flesh. Lunatic selection cheese, tissue, lactic secretions garnered of lesser sentient being. Bowels United State citizen harnessed heavy labor of process. Diet every spectrum culture across globe—based starches corn, rice, wheat, potato. All every citizen expected always dine, bowels tolerate infinite novelty perpetual introduced: fondue, dim sum, beef of Wellington. Intestines perennial challenged lasagna, burrito, Twinkie of Hostess.

All beauty created of the deity eventual to pass through American mouth, viscera, excreted anus.

Additional introduces food industry constant stream novel menu selections, every always touting new torture: steak tartare, marshmallow fluff, aspartame. Forever bombarding microwaves so burst kernel popcorns. Forever occupied electric ovens, burdened pizza pie consisting of solid ice.

Skinny claw chicken mother reach, snatch skin face cheek operative me, clamping skin, say, "I told Pygmy he could cook any ethnic thing he wanted, just so long as he didn't slaughter a goat in my kitchen."

Dawn of today, making most humble tone, voice of operative me request to prepare meal originating native homeland of this agent. Confront chicken host mother amid domain cooking appliance, larder too plentitude clashing foodstuffs.

Fashion face of operative me passable facsimile expression of caring, project demeanor juvenile affection. Perform best mimic begging sloth eye, stupid American child. Rational how host mother forever preparing so delicious meal, forever imprison place of stove, to repayment must this grateful agent instead suckle host family. Assemble consumables Thanksgiving.

Commencing ritual meal, pig dog brother load meat to own mouth, masticating roasted muscle fiber.

Hand lifted fork so close focus examine tines loaded beef, host mother poke own nose so inhale meat, say, "Did you hear?" Say, "They arrested Glen for abusing Trevor..." Tilt own torso vicinity host father, say whisper, "*Sex* abuse."

Twitching chicken mother say, "How Glen Stonefield could show his face in church, crying at his baby's coffin, I don't know." Say, "I mean, Trevor was brutally *sodomized*."

Delectable consumables supplemented abundant portion sodium chloride. Palatable savory beefs, pleasing grains rice with churned polyps potato impregnated dairy fats, all containing excessive sodium chloride. Generating great appetite of water, catalyst hunger of liquid gobbling vast beverage.

Pig dog swallowing, cat sister, cow father and chicken mother, all host family engaged feasting upon water.

Ingredient sodium chloride spur suffer starvation of water.

Nostril flared so deep sensate odor beef, mother peek into burden fork, say, "The autopsy, I guess it showed Trevor had *scars.*" Mother swivel skull so single nostril scenting morsel beef, say, "Inside his *bottom.*" Top and bottom incisor of mouth reach at fork, meet, sink, pinch strand single muscle fiber beef, string red beef sinew, say, "And the fissures or what all . . . they looked *fresh.*"

Cow father inhale odor emanating fork, say, "This ain't half-bad, but it doesn't taste like any beef I've ever eaten."

Explain this agent how no consume beef in homeland operative me. Culture of this agent holds beef solely as household mascot. Beloved pet.

Pig brother fork seize, halt middle of distance between plate and own mouth. Host brother eye ogle morsel meat, say, "This is *beef?*" Pig dog cast eye to rest upon this agent. Say, "*You* cooked this?"

Stealth cat sister say, "Why's it so *salty?*"

Explain how this agent initially required apprehend beef, extract collar with medals of identification, euthanasia painless utilizing Bird Wing Neck Twist, *zing-wring*, instant fast quick death. Subsequent dress beef carcass, removal paws, season meat, pan sear, bake four hundred degrees. Sprig rosemary.

Vast breathing cow father, squint smirk eye upon this agent, say, "Your English needs a little work." Say, "Cows don't have paws." Say, "We say *hooves* . . ."

Trapezius muscle host brother contract, lift shoulders so shrug near ears. Host brother remain consuming beef, say,

"Remember, little man, you're teaching me how to kill guys with my bare feet." Next now, face totter. Neck sway. Backbone drooping so face-plant pig dog nose deep plunge mashed-potato pile. Post crash land, skull remain mired, deep-breathing gravy lapsed comatose sleep. Mumble asleep through gravy, say, "I hope it's the Wilsons' 'beef.'" Drowning pig brother say, "I'm sick of hitting its shit with the lawn mower."

Next then wilts head chicken mother, dropping, settling pointed chin to rest upon cloth covering meal table. Head of cow father topple slow motioning more low, more low landing among own soiled plate.

Drinking water laced dense portion flunitrazepam, no-color pill of Rohypnol.

Water laced heavy solution gamma hydroxybutyric acid, no color liquid GHB.

Laced heavy suspension ketamine hydrochloride white-color powder.

Eye cover skins cat sister, skins flutter. Cover skins slide shut, flash open, flicker closed. Host sister shoulder neck melt, collapse face sideways until cheek flat laid atop table. Sister lips sputter, snort, sputter, say, "Pygmy, you *traitor . . .*" Say, "If I wake up pregnant, I'm *so* going to kick your ass . . ."

Stroking hair cat sister, dense hairs draping shape skull, lips operative me quote master prognosticator, vanguard pioneer Malcolm X, say, "'The future belongs to those who prepare for it today.'"

Delve hand operative me entering trouser cat sister, constraining denim warm of female thigh muscle. This agent extract cylinder for illumination, manipulate trigger except produce no brightness. Agitate, wag cylinder, only continue produce no brightness. Electric bulb intact. Surmise battery exhausted.

Recover out sister trouser jar containing salve black paint.

Next then, mission insist venture to beneath of family table, progressing upon kneel and hands operative me. Along floor, concealed within cloth table cover. Venture until position between kneels host mother, enveloping skull operative me within hemline mother skirt. Fingers operative me apprehending elastic edge, stitched decorative lace of host mother undergarment, stretch so enable withdrawal said apparel, reveal mature pubis. Shoulders operative me brace mother thighs more wide, enable fingers of this agent explore vaginal orifice. Discover ready lubricated copious flooded secretions natural mucus. Plundering depth vaginal vault, finger discover contain moderate missile polish plastic emitting gentle shiver vibration. Through tissue vault, contractions heart muscle faint, irregular. To removal, sliding, do battle vacuum so extract plastic missile until liberated flesh canal. Full evacuated, bright color yellow plastic. Twist until seam appear midway missile, spread wide, twist two threaded half-separated. Harvest cylinders battery.

Replace exhausted battery into missile. Seal two half together. Plunge missile so implanted hidden within birth passageway host mother.

Manipulate trigger, illuminate cylinder produce strength vast brightness. Valid battery.

This agent select spoon utensil, quickly stroke metal spoon abrading fabric tunic sleeve so polished most reflective. Position concave bowl spoon to mirror face operative me, reflection inverted, during apply layer black paint. Smudge black edging mouth this agent. Smear black surrounding eye, erasing inverted image operative me. Obliterate until visage operative me vanished.

Next now, position two finger operative me applied side

of cat sister neck. Detect sister heart muscle pumping weak, seldom. Upon removal fingers, remain on sister skin two oval blemish black paint, patterned friction ridges this agent. Position polish metal spoon within path cat sister nostril, fogged slight by flow breath steam, proof still alive.

Purse tight lips of this agent, knot lip muscles so tight as fist. Pressure fist of lips contacting lips of cat sister. Impact soft asleep lips host sister. Upon withdraw, this agent say, "Sole anything life guarantees humans to enjoy—eventual death." Say, "Nation of cat sister merely infinite contest determining most popular." Say, "American citizen all enslaved desiring affection, attention all fellow citizen."

Addicted adoration. Urgent need ardor from every direction.

Eyes operative me observe application black paint, smudged lips operative me, create black-colored lips upon cat sister. Next future event cat sister examine mirror, reflected there to discover lips kissed black.

Could be, this agent simply luggage sister until arrive sleeping platform, remove total apparel. Ready weapon operative me before helpless no-clothed vagina. Apply multitude flurry black kisses paint printed host sister nipples and vulva. Could be mount asleep vagina so implant seed.

Could be jawbone operative me chomp especial back molar this agent, liberate burst cyanide implanted hollow of bottom back tooth. Violate hollow. Expectorate cyanide into lip host sister.

With cat sister teetering edge death, sister heart slowed so flirting with damage to brain, so heavy sedative, current now bodes safe this agent offer announcement. Lips operative me kissed red, leaving own black stain behind, this agent say, "If able attain love only sister..."

Say, "Would this agent never all other love require..."

Instead impregnate cat sister, instead cyanide assassinate, feet operative me make small parade to stance beside asleep host father. Fingers of this agent entwine among head hairs cow father, yank so lift host father skull from table. As obstacle, head hair peel free of scalp. Revealed strands as artificial. As solution, two fingers operative me hook nostrils, anchored so pull to make skull lifted. Father mouth trumpet snore at roof. With chest of father blouse exposed, this agent purloin security badge.

Utilizing polish metal spoon, one hand operative me hooking nostrils so lift head, opposite hand operative me wedge spoon along bottom margin prosthetic eye. Edge spoon bowl sunken deep divide between eyeball and flesh socket of father skull. Wiggle wedging spoon more deep, this agent apply increase pressure handle of utensil, pressure causing eyeball bulge. Scooping spoon swell eyeball to escape, ready emerge out socket with increase of gentle push. Eye much realistic, cracked broken into countless tunnel for red blood. Iris crafted every shade green.

"Pygmy?" voice say, female voice.

Host father artificial eye ready about almost to pop free. Bulge before crucial moment eyeball rupture.

Cat sister head slight lifted off table, squinting so focus host sister eyes, say black lips, "That's his *good* eye..." Sister say, eye cover skins sliding closed, say, "Try the *other* one..." Say, "Dipshit." Host sister skull resettle upon table surface, say muffled, "Steal me some printer cartridges, okay?" Lapsed next then, bewitched of sedative, fallen full submerged sleep.

Possible could be cat sister perceived oral profession love of this agent.

Could be host sister aware during confessed most worst secret operative me.

Quote say, "The future belongs to those who prepare for it today."

Next then, new position spoon opposite eye of host father. Plunge to wedge between bottom edge eyeball and socket. Apply pressure spoon handle.

Within head operative me, in secret recite, say, *Strontium...plutonium...uranium...*

Same now, prosthetic glass eye erupt rattling ricochet side water glass, rebound skull asleep pig brother, splash amidst sodium chloride sauce pulverized potatoes, green eyeball gazing contempt at direction this agent.

Dispatch
Twenty-fifth

Begins here twenty-fifth account of operative me, agent number 67, recalling covert training of past formative year ▒▒▒▒▒. This today, acquire stealth battle philosophy espoused top esteemed field marshal ▒▒▒▒▒. Explained secret espionage purpose of operative genitals, all agents, advancing world power of homeland ▒▒▒▒▒.

For official record, repeat recounting here early childhood history. For reinforce early important training of this agent, this former now aged eight years since birth.

According famed field marshal, all entire member United State adults, all most savor sexual intercourse atop children. American citizen drooling pedophile famished for consume tender child genital.

During revered distinguished field marshal present lecture, assuming stance at focus all student. Black-color boot rooted wide apart, uniform trouser tucked interior top collar laced boot per regulation. Field marshal clasp both own hand so folded behind back. Black uniform tunic plated many gold medals layering location above heart muscle. Plated thick metal. Medals bravery. Rewarded medals misery. Voice revered field marshal, trumpet lesson word. Eye cover skins no ever action blink.

Attentive seated, operatives Magda, Tanek, Otto, all agent, Tibor, Bokara, Ling. Former now, during field marshal make small parade so penetrate chamber, all agent speaking single voice, say, "Greetings, esteemed most revered educator."

Unite wave of voice, all operative say, "Accept, please, our gratitude for the wisdom you impart."

Field marshal bow head.

Operative all bow head.

According explain field marshal, former past history, all American citizen hidden homosexual. All hungering clandestine masturbation within orifice fellow citizen identical gender. Best most enjoy so private mutual degradation. Thus for top method gain access government, attain power over individual, must operative merely engage enjoined sodomy within American. Next then, subsequent threaten expose said citizen as surreptitious pervert. Under past strategy must victim supply said operative government confidential information, supply currency. Fulfill all such requests from terror for being named public sodomite.

During recite profound lecture, hands acclaimed field marshal manipulate own buckle of belt. Free belt. Extract belt leather strap out entire waistband trouser. Hand fingers clutch fabric of tunic where constrained within waistband. Draw tunic hem upward until free of trouser, tails tunic hang loose, marred many wrinkle.

Distinguished field marshal recounting valuable lesson gleaned under countless painful violation. Mounted beneath degrading copulations committed vast number American senator, governor of state, chairman joint chiefs of staff.

Heart muscle plated gold medals commending field marshal endurance so humiliation.

Next now, kneel of field marshal flex, lower torso so hands able loosen laces one boot. Hands loosen laces second boot. Feet revered field marshal lift so step free, abandoning both empty boot.

Since modern era, explain renowned field marshal, depraved United State nation embraces such degenerates. America boasts frequent vast public parade for flaunting sodomy. Generating no shame, no afraid, historical threaten exposure no longer effective means extortion.

Hand fingers wise field marshal liberate waistband closure. Legs step free uniform trouser. Make careful folded crease of trouser, place atop boots. Place boot and trouser aside.

"Important," say acclaimed field marshal, appareled solely tunic, bikini inner pants. Bikini inner pants fashioned olive drab color. Revealing narrow leg limbs, luxuriant with dense hairs, say, "Subsequent to digital stimulation American anus, must always every operative launder hands..."

Offer all operative latex hand coverings. Offer gelatin lubricant transparent of no color.

Field marshal exclaim how American devils no squeamish of any possible genital acts. Forever tunneling rodents inserted rectums even top famous movie actors. Phallus and orifice United State vipers forever textured plentitude numerous nodules, knobby as sea creature, anemone or sea cucumber, so crowded dense carpeted with venereal wart.

"Resulting such frequent abuse," say field marshal, "American orifice perennial diseased." Say, "Vector always infection."

Hands respected field marshal no yet remove own bikini.

Tanek pass latex hand covers, pass gelatin, distributed Otto, distributed Sheena, Oleg, Vaky until all operative so equipped.

In secret, interior thinking machine operative me, no voice, say, *Carbon ... cerium ... cesium ...*

"Most crucial," say field marshal, "able instant fast locate prostate or urethral sponge for vigorous stimulate." Bikini remain intact, masking genital, field marshal say, "American nation suffer culture of desire..."

According lecture, entire effort United State to incite desire, inflict want, inspire demand. Every today American vermin offered too many objects for acquire. Offered too numerous formula for succeed. Too vast selection religion, vocation, lifestyle. No ever able make choice. Resulting outcome no happiness, forever striving pursuit next objective. Next possession or experience or reproductive mate.

Finger engaging elastic waistband bikini, field marshal explain superior nature this homeland. Here, the state encourages no option exist. Limit each possible choice every citizen. Provide best simple selection of residence, education, career, partner. Wise, knowledgeable state officials permit no citizen confused by stress of opportunity, stress of surprise, or lofty aspiration. So inflict greater happiness, this homeland channel all citizen routed along single path correct life. Solely most noble purpose entire life energy. No clutter of wide variety. No turmoil generated by personal choice.

"Future today," say field marshal, "to demonstrate correct method harbor condom concealed within face cheek so able utilize during fellatio American president." Say, "Thus containing explosion president seed." Say, "Most effective preserving wardrobe."

Field marshal quote eminent military general, courageous visionary Idi Amin, say, "'You cannot run faster than a bullet.'"

This today, hands field marshal engage elastic of bikini. Extract one thigh out. Extract second thigh so reveal most illustrious genital dangling below tails of tunic, chest remain clad many gold medal. For succeed in America must operative become accomplished top sexual participant. In demon culture of despotic United States must agents attain status of object exciting most desire.

Neck respected field marshal rotate. Shoulder rotate. Torso rotate to make entire body expose withered buttock at assembly operative in training.

Breath this agent limited tiny inhale, tiny exhale, repeat rapid. Rapid ripple heart muscle. Hands operative me tremble tiny twitch. In secret terror, operative me recite, no voice, say, *Cobalt ... copper ... curium ...*

This today, study location prostate. Next today, clitoris. Second next today, nipples. Study stimulation lips. Stimulation scrotum. Craft best effective service of pervert penis and vagina. In vengeance against American predators must total operative graduate expert in pleasing all pedophile for extortion.

All operative witness wrinkled pucker, horror shit eye leading field marshal, constrict small circumference. Squeeze tight knot. Next expand, relax so squirming red color muscle achieve full blossom. Repeat constrict, then relax, so pulse.

Viscera operative me convulse, spasm. Esophagus flooded bitter taste much digestive acid. Apple of Adam jump with effort swallow such stomach bile.

This homeland, total freedom of no options. Solely inevitable duty: doom.

Could be legs operative me spring out desk seat, land killing Kangaroo Kick, *thug-thump*, so render field marshal into coma, allow this agent escape classroom. Flee state.

Quote, "You cannot run faster than a bullet."

This agent fated forever enjoy comfort of such trap.

All every student instant quick donning latex hand cover during field marshal squat so expose pink pleated tissue today lesson. Grant access. Same now, voice field marshal summon name initial agent to volunteer.

Dispatch
Twenty-sixth

Begins here twenty-sixth account of operative me, agent number 67, attending alive living torture Junior Swing Choir. Have initiated construction weapon of mass destruction ████████. Crafting success recent foray for obtain deadly neurotoxin ████████. Effective dispersal method ████████. For official record, current now, ape mimic joyous facial expression fellow student during bellow propaganda lyrics. All lauding agrarian United State deemed Oklahoma, primitive environment employing equine labor for drag wheeled conveyance despoiled with superfluous decorative fringe.

This agent stance among ranked students, multiple row sorted tone of voice, segregated, this agent directed endure amidst shrill mouths female student. Voice operative me directed bellow solely most squeal-pitched portions each lyric. Describe glowing carriage desecrated with hang of fringe. Honey lambs. Stalk cereal corn grown height comparable eyeball of pachyderm. Insane garbage lyrics. Directed no scowl during bellow such lunatic word.

For official record, most big words printed ink across American news broadsheet this today announce male parentage Trevor Stonefield arrested by state, charged sodomize abuse own son. Coarse newsprint image present Glen Stonefield eyes bleeding copious water during placed in bondage by law officers. Female Stonefield in addition bleeding eye water, flat palms female hands pressured both face cheeks male, female calf muscles contracted so balance atop toes, fisted lips reach until almost moment contact lips male parentage. Male Stonefield strain against bonds. Female hands securing final moment male face.

During bellow attributes Oklahoma state, conceal newsprint folded said photograph within trouser operative me. Fingers this agent reading by touch, feel ink faces grieving parentage. In secret, lips operative me say, within head quote ruthless leader, merciless tyrant Adolf Hitler, say, "It is not truth that matters, but victory."

Drowned among wail of praise for waving wheat, cattle stance so mimic statues, voice whisper say, "Pygmy?"

Female voice, host sister, stealth cat, say, "The other night?" Say, "On Thanksgiving..." Sister stance immediate behind this agent, crowded deep within squeal-pitched female voices. Sweet exhale of sister buffeting ear this agent.

Sister voice camouflaged amid din, so many boasting glory city of Kansas. How such modern. Screaming all conceit. American arrogance. Much booming pride for skyscraping building consisting seven floor. How toilet contained interior residence, no mere outdoors pit excavated for collect feces. Merry American youth trumpet much egotism such recent progress.

Drowned flurry such compulsory celebration propaganda, cat sister say, "I mean, did you swipe the printer cartridges I asked for?"

No rotating neck so contact eyes of cat sister, this agent tilt skull forward, tilt back, repeat to make head meaning "yes." Finger concealed within trouser, stroking photo moist faces Stonefield parentage. In addition, stroking turgid rise weapon this agent.

Sweet exhale sister voice say, "I think you gave my brother

brain damage from all those drugs . . ." Say, "But with him it's hard to tell."

Surround this agent, bellowing skulls multiple viable reproductive female: former delegate Norway, former lady delegate Palau, delegate Zambia. Negroid. Mongoloid. Caucasoid. Madam Party Pillows. Madam Blouse Bunnies. Every vagina hoarding treasure trove precious cargo female eggs starved for male seed. Such army future soldier, doctor, political operative, civil engineer, suppressed in order females scream yodel touting vast cultural advancement city of Kansas. Boast over no clothed degenerate burlesque dance. Public telephone.

So corrupt evil vile American liberal culture. Such United State pretension.

Next then, other female voice, whisper say, "Attention, comrade."

Voice operative Magda, made stance to rear this agent. Ear opposite cat sister, Magda say, "Required must make test utilizing deadly neurotoxin, prior Operation Havoc . . ."

Same now, cat sister say, "Did you *kiss* me?" Say, "I mean, while I was asleep?"

Voice Magda, breath say, "Required expose test subject to gauge effects fatal toxin."

Scent cat sister breath, sweet of latex chew gum. Scent Magda breath, the odor of comrade stale teeth.

Same now, cat sister say, "I mean, I woke up and my lips were black . . ."

Amid youth crooning propaganda song, numerous male suffer fracture arm, limb hung sling, cast layers heavy fiberglass. All every male student requesting this agent inscribe message atop surface new fiberglass limb. Instruct operative me inscribe, "To my best bud . . ." Or, "To the number one member of my crew..." Crippled youth scampering so able provide elements science fair project this agent. Enamored youth provisioning bomb container, ingredient explosion, method ignition. Each sourcing different element, timing device, or brown packaging. No student able surmise total purpose every combined such innocuous articles: metal canister, clock radio, potassium nitrate, adhesive tape.

"Another thing is..." say cat sister, "my mom found black fingerprints on her pussy, and she's blaming me."

In secret, this agent reciting within head, no voice, say, *Tin...titanium...tungsten...*

Host sister say, "If you swiped my mom's batteries, you need to come clean."

Magda breath say, "Attention, comrade." Say, "Mission directive communicate target for purpose testing neurotoxin..."

Remain all fellow student warble evoking pride how grand state of Oklahoma. During prideful yodel, student keyboard tiny message. Different student thumb strategy electric competition contained colored lights of tiny box. Different student decipher text received on private screen. Witness broadcast narrative displayed tiny screen. Hunt images many professional actors engaged in reproductive acts, multiple variety couplings, coital position, teach breeding instruction. However in error, instructors always depositing seed upon mammary glands or face cheeks or anus female partner, idiot American males never successful to breeding offspring.

Always attempting fertilize. Never succeed. Such poor role model.

Always extract weapon total wrong moment.

Fellow operative present attend Junior Swing Choir—Tibor, Mang, Chernok, Tanek, Otto, and Vaky—all cast eyeball so rest upon this agent. Almost total population male students this today appareled black tunic printed English letter words "Property of Jesus." When event contact eye operative me, such student collapse half face to make wink eye. Remain croon lyrics propaganda.

Cat sister breath, sweet breath perch upon shoulder operative me, billow into ear, say, "I'll make you a deal, Pygmy." Say, "Keep your paws out of my mom's pussy, and I'll show you my project for the science fair . . ."

Reiterate breath operative Magda, whisper say no sufficient fellow operative mere execute top profound science fair project, brilliant inspired project, must in addition sabotage projects created competing students. Ensure victory operative projects local, preliminary regional competitions, Magda remind. Guarantee admission of deadly projects into national finals staged Washington, D.C., in capital of devil nation. Operation Havoc assured most worst impact, *zing-pow-wham*, create infinite damage dead.

Vengeance upon American vipers.

Within thinking machine this agent, picture parentage operative me, final mental narrative, reciting, *Xenon . . . ytterbium . . . yttrium . . .*

Within trouser operative me, folded faces Stonefield parentage, bleeding water. Could be grieving family imprisoned, shunned, rejected out community worship shrine. Devil Tony. Finger of this agent smudged black from so prolonged contact ink. Sullied. Still, no able newsprint discard.

Quote, "It is not truth that matters, but victory."

Next then, lips operative Magda hover at aural canal this agent, whisper say target of testing neurotoxin. Announce name, human determined suffer as test subject.

White rodent to be erased.

During all everything detail of scene, lips operative me mouth words praising state. Hymn Oklahoma. Teeth and tongue muscle of this agent describe lyrics during issue no sound. Craft shape song words, except no voice. Solely mime involvement. Register opportunity inspect science project offered cat sister. Accept name test subject Magda determined must die. However, face of this agent merely pretend happy participation.

Dispatch
Twenty-seventh

Begins here twenty-seventh account of operative me, agent number 67, repeat attending student mating ritual located darkened sports arena of education facility. Night of today ██████. Subjected onslaught of high-sucrose song lyric, musical corn syrup, repetitive sentiments, timed tempo mimicking quickened intercourse during moments prior to erect penis spewing seed. Alternately, more slower music permit prolonged engagement foreplay whereby pubescent males abrade females utilizing erect phalli.

For official record, ranked present Madam Sweater Meats, accompanied esteemed Lady Party Pillows. Ranked along opposite edge basketball wood, all female offering on display exposed midriff boasting musculature dimpled umbilical scar. Dark hollow each scar adorned decorative jewel. Secreted there, minute loop crafted of precious metal. Lady delegate Nepal, lady delegate Burundi, brazenly undulate such loins honed of solid muscle, flaunting smooth flanks composed no blemished skin atop much skeletal muscle.

All female students having before deflected reproductive advances of this agent. On occasion previous student ritual, all refuse for incubate viable offspring operative me. Rejecting, yet scarcely conceal vast wealth clitori and fragrant nipple.

Amid din clamorous ritual music, obscured dim lighting of basketball arena, approaching now operative Sheena, agent

7, bidding say, "Comrade." Say, "For best interest Operation Havoc, request engage making ritual American sexual dance." Sheena extend own hand, grasping clutch of cold iron around wrist of operative me. Sheena compel this agent follow, penetrating among gyrating ritual, during Sheena say, "Simply mount as would typical American female vessel."

Positioned within epicenter student mating partners, feet of operative me step tentative to discovering music pace. Groin of operative me thrust in duplicate American males peerage, battering clothed groin of Sheena, during hands of this agent thrash for randomly fill surrounding space.

So busy occupied, this agent no aware how becoming surrounded among fellow operatives, Mang, Tanek, Bokara. Embittered against this agent following battle of dodged balls. All positioned as clock face encircling this agent, Tibor at one o'clock preparing for execute Bashing Baboon maneuver. Mang assume stance at seven-o'clock position, readied for launching cruel Manatee Murder Maul. Ling at eleven o'clock. Chernok at four o'clock. Tanek postured to initiate brutal Monkey Mash. Fist and elbow of Otto preparing much fatal Pounding Panda.

Ranked eight o'clock, two o'clock, ten o'clock entirely besieging all side operative me.

Each fellow operative commence land violent crippling strike attempt upon this agent. All endeavor for impact vicious pounding elbow blast for immediate dispatching life of operative me.

Entire vision this agent filled slashing of chop hands. Filled deadly swipe of murdering kick feet. Blurred wind of many infinite such deadly assaults. Poking finger. Butting heads. Entire physical limbs of this agent dodging thrown fist, quick speed, thwarting swung foot. Spinning all direction, electric bolt fast, reflex of operative me enlist prior training history so block blow from one o'clock, stop impact from eight o'clock, sidestep Lashing Lion.

During churned darkness, slashing wind generated so many dangerous assassination, amidst storm perspiration, panting exhales such strenuous exertions, operative Sheena say, "Comrade." Say, "No shall betray sacred mission of Operation Havoc."

From behind cannonball of own clenched fist, operative Oleg say, "Ready self for die, comrade!"

During same now, American student surrender ritual floor. Student adolescents recede until merely observing melee lashing leg and arm. Flashing repeated moments such almost murder of operative me.

Next now, female voice say, "What a weird *dance...*" Voice Madam Chesticles say, "It's some weird native *rain* dance they're doing!"

Madam Butter Bags say, "Cool!" Commence attempt duplicate fist punching nothing, heel kicking nothing. Every female enrolled flurry such mimicry. Aping all ruthless battle technique. Next then, inflicting own svelte bodies among throng killer operatives. Encroaching nubile student females, jabbing lady elbows so displace murderous agents. In so doing, fertile adolescent females advance upon operative me, encircling this agent until constitute entire wall such desirable flesh, bulwark for separate from all attackers.

Succulent barrier much thrusting mammary glands shield operative me, swinging lady buttocks thwart further attacks. Insulate, exclude from further aggression fellow operative. Lady females whip with long lengths own head hair, much health hair, dense weight, wicked flogging. Engorged glands pummeling deadly agents into retreat.

Encapsulated within deep interior, resulting warm sanctuary smooth lady flesh, flashing lips, licking tongues, total best arrayed selection robust genetic material, this agent continue gyrate ensured for moment much safe.

Dispatch
Twenty-eighth

Begins here twenty-eighth account of operative me, agent number 67, on covert mission, foray for visit religion propaganda distribution outlet of city ███████. Purpose test effect neurotoxin ███████. This today no Sabbath. Fatal toxin intended victim test subject ███████.

Arrive solitary this agent, discover door worship shrine secured sturdy mechanism lock. Standard type dead-bolt lock. Eyes operative me cast sideways one direction, cast second direction so ensure street vacant possible witness. Solely aware this agent chilled movement November wind. Stratus cloud suggest bleak underbelly, black underside ready deposit frozen precipitation. Every all credible witness in attendance education lessons, could be laboring location employment, or entrapped by daylight programming television viewing appliance.

For official record, teeth operative me masticate own lips this agent so flooded blood glow, swollen lips enticing slight minor edema. Produce succulent seducing child lips no able pedophile to resist. Fingers operative me clamp skin own face cheeks, suffusing radiant blood glow. Effect face innocent child anxious yearning for shed virginity.

Instant fast quick, hands operative me extract thin stylus out trouser, invade orifice of key so able rape lock. Jab violent tiny hole. Twist, apply pressure interior tight slot. Abuse until lock, bolt tripped. Door no healed in wall. Eyes revisit no possible witness, feet of this agent venture within worship shrine. Lock door so sealed this agent on interior.

No present rotting alive skeleton corpse Doris Lilly. No present fellow citizens congregation.

Worship shrine empty of all sound. Full silent. Dim all illumination excepting tainted sunlight tinted red colors, deep blue colors stained window glass. Composing sanctuary perpetual twilight.

Honeyed reek numerous genital chrysanthemum plant. Vivid hue carnation plant penis and vagina. Drenched pigment window glass. Render every inhale breath rich rainbow-tinted, perfumed odor.

Cylinders paraffin, burning string extinguished.

Only sole witness, fake statue plaster dead male, fake torture dead on two crossed stick, fake blood painted red hand and foot.

Feet operative me make small parade so approach worship altar, water bin wherein Magda attempted drown Reverend Tony. Devil Tony. At stance below feet plaster male bleeding red paint, this agent flex own legs so crouch. Next now, explode leg muscles, *zing-spring*, Leaping Lemur, swipe hand for grasp plaster feet.

For official record, no successful. Repeat make Leaping Lemur.

No successful reach statue mounted so high on wall.

Bouncing within trouser, glass vial deadly neurotoxin.

Could be this agent introduce toxin to water bin, assassinate future all initiated by devil Tony. Could be taint book scriptures, Holy Bible, for exterminate all reader. Possible poison shared chalice, lip of goblet utilized total congregants during wine ritual, soil so all ingest noxious toxin.

Heinous acts. Earn this agent horror future trauma cancer,

aircraft accident already fated. Craft deserving this agent suffer such torture and murder premeditated by top deity.

Recite in secret, this agent quote magnificent statesman, best top bold magistrate Joseph Stalin, say, "A single death is a tragedy; a million deaths is a statistic."

Legs compressed, this agent attempt additional Leaping Lemur. Hands grasp plaster statue toes, grasp plaster spike hammered through foot. Arm muscle operative me lift self, climb statue where mounted most height shrine wall. Naked torture male thick layered much dust. This agent smudged, suffocated such dense dust during scale enormous plaster figure. Each plaster thigh the equivalent caliber 914-millimeter "Little David," siege mortar of United State artillery. Plaster statue arm matched caliber 800-millimeter "Schwerer Gustav," siege mortar Nazi Germany.

Shinny up same as climb main trunk, limb *Castanea dentata*.

Crawling, scaling, gripping handhold, toehold wedged between musculature definition tortured statue, this agent climb legs, slink sliding along plaster groin, gain surmount loincloth. Hand operative me hook all fingers into vast cavity statue navel. Extend reach so able clasp handhold of huge plaster nipple. Statue feature cavern of fake wound, spear hacked deep into left side torso, cruel mortal wound brimming red paint inflicted below rib cage left-side abdomen. For avoid fatigue, seek respite, this agent attain cavern of spear wound. Seated within hollow of laceration, adjacent exposed plaster viscera, legs operative me dangle, eyes able visible entire wide acreage worship shrine. All seat. Location now absent casket Trevor Stonefield.

Heart muscle operative me rapid pump subside. Achieve rest. From lofty height mortal wound, experience honeyed

reek, rich red, gold color, royal blue color sanctuary atmosphere. Vast space swimming full such jewel window color.
Perfumed stench.

Repeat effort scaling plaster male, emerge out wound so
gripping knob giant nipple. Reaching hand so grasp clavicle.
Dragging this agent ever more high. Find secure toehold between ribs emaciated statue. Find toehold within many curls
plaster hair of chest. Find handhold among curls plaster male
beard. Hands operative me gripping fake hat woven strands
thick plaster thorns, haul hips of this agent so seated atop
plaster deltoid.

For official record, this agent perched upon right-hand
shoulder plaster male spiked to crossed sticks wood. Legs operative me dangle, swing down vast pectoral muscle, heels
kicking clavicle. Lips operative me level with aural canal plaster head. Shell of ear cartilage big sized enough could entire
arm operative me delve inside.

Sudden sound mystery voice. Occur loud shout.

Voice say, out cavern audience seating, male voice shout,
"What the fuck are you up to?"

Voice, devil Tony. Making parade along main aisle, approaching position directly below plaster statue, devil Tony
say, "This happens to be *my* church..." Say, "We keep those
doors *locked* for a reason."

Voice devil Tony rasp, coarse subsequent subdural hematoma resulting attack operative Magda. Caused screaming
during full submerged water bin.

Buttocks operative me seated, lips of this agent remain
sealed.

"If this is some kind of political protest," say devil Tony,
"you are way off base." From stance below statue, Tony head
tilted back, peering up, say, "I'll call the police, I swear."

Devil Tony. This agent. Entire scene suspended atmosphere silent, perfume smell, stained colors.

Arms folded so cross own chest, devil Tony tap floor with toe one shoe, say, "Don't think I won't, mister." Say, "I'm not bluffing."

In secret, this agent reciting whisper, say, "Neon . . . neptunium . . . nickel . . ." Whisper say into right-hand ear torture male, yawning plaster ear, whisper, "Platinum . . . polonium . . . potassium . . ."

Concealed within trouser operative me, neurotoxin requiring test. Pig of Guinea.

Next then, devil Tony commence pace small parade, one direction, opposite direction, pacing as sentry far below statue. Pacing, say, "You're not going to blackmail me." Say, "It's not my fault, what happened . . ."

Pacing cease, devil Tony flex both leg, sink so kneel at feet great statue. Both hand gripped fist. Shake both fist at statue face, say, "She told me she was *eighteen*." Say, "*She told me she was on the pill.*"

Fisting this atmosphere sweet scent, luminous gold color, spittle flashing red, blue, yellow colors, devil Tony say, "*How's it my fault if the bitch can't speak decent English?*"

Such remark reference agent 36. Operative Magda.

Concealed with trouser operative me, noxious toxin. Folded newsprint photograph depicting imprisoned grieving Stonefield parentage. Remaining soiled paper dollars confiscated rape of clear-yellow bully.

Operative Magda gestating fetus fathered . . . devil Tony.

State-designated reproductive partner this agent.

Quote, "A single death is a tragedy; a million deaths is a statistic."

Eyes devil Tony begging response, starving of mercy, peering up, Tony say, "Hey!" Say, "I'm still *down* here." Say, "Can you at least give me a *sign?*"

Ensconced right-hand shoulder supreme plaster male, this agent extract glass vial out trouser. Extract currency bill former of clear-yellow bully. At final, extract wadded fabric white color, circled elastic three openings, knit cotton fabric—inner pants former occupied groin operative Magda. Soiled blood at junction two thigh, stiff from dried patches, male seed stain pubis. Hand operative me, finger this agent release inner bikini pants so plummet, dropping straight distance, fluttering, drifting shift white color through red light, yellow light, gold, spattered blood former Magda maidenhead. Crusted leakage excess devil seed.

Where seated atop lofty shoulder, red paint out hat of thorns, paint bleed wide stripes down plaster face cheek, pale plaster neck dead statue.

During fall inner pants, settle through luscious scent, sugary reek plant life. Descend until landed soft pile adjacent kneel devil Tony. Devil legs stand, venture stride, flex, stoop so hand seize impregnated bikini pants, instant fast conceal within fist. Stabbing bikini fist upward, jabbing eyes at statue, neck craned backward so expose tender windpipe, devil Tony say, "These prove *nothing . . .*"

Inner pants granted this agent during Junior Swing Choir, given of Magda last today.

Covert next then, devil clutch fist containing inner pants. Duck chin and position soiled pants at nostril. Almost hidden, in secret devil predator inhale pubis scent. Lingering cologne demolished hymen. Small tainted trace amount neural toxin for test.

Quote, "A single death is a tragedy; a million deaths is a statistic."

Same now, devil Tony face skin bleach pallid. Skull topple atop slack neck. Heavy skull drag down total cadaver, entire skeleton fold to floor worship shrine. Devil deleted. Solely muscle random twitch. Seeping tiny trickle blood both ear.

White rodent erased.

Dispatch
Twenty-ninth

Begins here twenty-ninth account of operative me, agent number 67, competing first-round preliminaries National Science Fair, regional chapter of state ▓▓▓▓▓. Top important priority: project operative me judged most best, deemed worthy progress next succeeding level science fair located metropolitan area ▓▓▓▓▓. Allow this agent detonate righteous vengeance accompanied along operative Tanek, Magda, Chernok, Ling, all agent, on behalf glorious homeland ▓▓▓▓▓.

Science fair competition consist judges, top esteemed academic scholar, respected instructor, tour amongst project, stop so listen during each young entrant describe. Each judge frequent consult wristwatch. Often mask with open hand, stifle stretched mouth of yawn.

For official record, decoy science project operative me staged so appear merely demonstration copackaged DNA recombinant intermolecular template-switching subsequent recombinant strain viral reptile RNA. Craft this agent placard, pink-color cardboard lettered English words "Path to Permanent Global Peace." Outlining recombination rates, evolution system based necrosis reptile RNA. Such elementary. So simple easily infant able comprehend. Experiment such softball prompt operative Oleg guffaw. Tibor snickering.

Location event this today, regional competition projects National Science Fair displayed same sports arena wherein original this agent attended mating ritual gyrating among music, introduced Madam Milk Makers. Next then, staged this here, Model United Nation. Most recent, battle of dodging balls.

Lips operative me explain method surefire bring about global peace. Resolve significant world political conflict. Simply analyze human genome for identify traits linked violence, conflict associated reptilian brain stem. Offer adequate treatment so suppress impulse hostility. Isolate out all individual predisposed aggression for appropriate gene therapy. Eradicate every strife within single generation humanity. Craft world happy sunshine peace. Beneficent lovely flower peace.

Offer face operative me, shining facsimile expression smile.

Among gullible judges, professor say, "World peace?" Bobbing skull to make head meaning "yes," say, "Peace is *really* good."

Secret within thinking machine operative me, no voice, quote profound genius, generous mentor Leon Trotsky, say, "On every side, the slug humanitarianism leaves its slimy trail, obscuring the function of intelligence and atrophying emotion."

In actual, project vessel labeled "Peace Machine," for reality to deliver quantity neurotoxin deep within core United State capital city, *kah-blam*, trigger dispersal, no relenting murder countless American vermin.

Present cat sister, keyboarding small telephone, apply to own ear. Pressuring phone to ear, say, "Come on, Dad . . ." Say, "Answer your *phone*."

Once depraved tyrants of America fatal extinguished, reign future then world at peace.

As per decreed operative Magda, all opposing projects generated local student, such projects rudely sabotaged. For ensure success Operation Havoc. Construction simple electromagnetic purposed for gather wire fashioned clipping paper—exhibit foiled with inclusion clips composed solely plastic. Scale model volcano no erupt after provisioned with ingredients phosgene gas, nearly exhibit deadly suffocate young geologist.

All competitor frantic laboring repair botched project. Failed chemist. Would-be biologist.

Solely cat sister beam confident of project. Host sister remain stance adjacent folded table, own placard lettered boasting merits invention. Sister contract trapezius muscle so shoulder shrug up around ears, say, "It started as a regular gift for Mother's Day." Say, "Then kind of spun out of control..."

Cat sister eye tiny telephone, say, "Dad *promised* to be here..." Say, "Where is he?"

Beginning moment lips operative me, during give oral lecture explaining DNA project, professor eye clouded cataract indicating boredom. Muscle eye no focused. Pupil eye wandering direction knitted sweater, leader of cheers, Madam Chesticles. Professor ogle tunic Madam Sweater Meats.

Other professor blink eye cover skins, draw brow pinched in center, say, "Hey, aren't you the kid saved everybody from the crazy shooter?"

Peace lecture operative me interrupted.

Other inspecting professor point writing instrument, say, "You're Pygmy?"

Fellow professor say, "From the TV...?" Offer own ballpoint pen, offer tablet filled notes compare competing science project, say, "Can I have your autograph?"

Hand operative me make signature atop sheet of paper. Signature second sheet. Signature all sheet as "Pygmy," despite no actual name this agent. Assemblage professor, learned band judges dismiss science project operative me. Instead, grasp hand of this agent. Agitate hand. Make small parade so examine next exhibition.

Next science project, plant life produced hydroponics garden exposed as *Cannabis sativa*. Officers of law summoned. Loud protesting own innocence, student botanist taken custody, rapid spirited out venue. Sabotage successful.

From distance exhibition floor, observe operative Otto beaming gleeful smile. So prideful such clever sabotage.

Next, parade learned academics arrive experiment invented stealth cat sister. Rested atop table, displayed moderate missile comparable light mortar round Japan artillery, caliber fifty-millimeter Type 89 "leg" mortar shell. Missile encased skin pink-color plastic. Smooth polished. Painted letter across placard, written: "Bliss 2.0."

Say host cat sister, "May I introduce the next generation in complete happiness..." Hands sister lift missile, brandish before attention all judge, explain as miracle prosthetic phallus. Appliance phallus able wireless attach World Wide Web, download supplement software, upgrade programming. Tailor for simulate multiple sexual scenario ranging tentative penis wielded adolescent youth to top range mindless rape platoon enemy army soldier. Masquerade genital member any global archetype. Simply user submit code of scenario so activate.

In addition, boast phallus able adjust surface temperature. Wide variety warmth for chilled circumstance. For heated weather, offered phallus able chill itself, assist lower core temperature of user. Explain sister, top best cost savings compared expense for operate conventional central air-condition.

As bonus feature, phallus include ability perform recorded music. Capacity storage more than fifteen hundred song file, audio book, academic classroom lecture, religious reading. Synchronize stimulation vibrate so matched music. Suggested possible able educate user, imprint wisdom facts, knowledge during embedded shuddering consumer pelvis.

"Plus..." say cat sister, closing eye cover skins for effect, tilting head meaning "yes," say, "the wipe-clean finish is antimicrobial." Say, "And... it's the last *anything* you'll ever need inside yourself."

"What?" say learned judge, make small laugh, say, "It's not powered by nuclear fusion?"

Cat sister offer weak smile, say, "We'll be launching that product feature with Bliss 2.1."

Explain host sister, phallus total compatible either IBM or Apple platform.

Contain global positioning sensor so forever orient by satellite.

Automatic relay fault codes, conduct own systems check each usage. Time-delayed activation so function as clock of alarms. Converse, programmed stop own operation automatic once user metabolism indicates asleep.

Other standard feature, phallus employs conductivity of skin to measure user glucose levels, monitor electrolytes bodily fluids, test serum cholesterol. Regulate cycle ovulation. Enhance memory. Coordinate wardrobe. Increase automobile gasoline mileage.

In secret this agent reciting, no voice, say, *Erbium... europium ... fermium...*

Total top easy host sister to be awarded best prize of science fair. Not this agent. Instead cat sister journey so compete finals competition, city of Washington, district of Columbia. Thwart objective Operation Havoc.

Anxious observant all operative, Bokara, Sheena, Mang, frightened such miracle device garner most top award, usurp opportunity advance to national competition.

Next then, professor request demonstrate appliance. Demand show how activate miracle phallus.

Focused amid all present watching, cat sister manipulate missile, handle hidden control appliance base, activate mechanism for commence pink-color plastic transform more shade pink, more darker pink, color shading red. Next then, phallus pulse surge, vibrate, quiver, shiver. Invention shake, oscillate, tremble. Project joggle, jiggle, flutter. Emerge sweet melody music, trill melodious tune.

Face numerous professor fashion wide smile.

Cat sister smile.

Sudden now, phallus increase degree jostle. Machinery convulse, quake, jolt. Thin ribbon smoke, white smoke stray out plastic shell. Smoking phallus jump, caper, jerk, issuing dark smoke, black smoke.

Crowd all present retreat one stride, recede safe distance during phallus sprout miniature flame, red, yellow, blue flame. Sound screaming wail, no pretty music. Wailing demon phallus spring from table, bolt about exhibition floor, pursuing terrified judges. Trailing acrid black smoke, comet tail orange flames, screaming killer phallus spit molten plastic, pounce in chase wailing students. Stalk howling youth. Squalling inflamed phallus hunt squealing children.

Same now, tiny telephone host sister sound ring. Adamant ring.

Phone applied ear, cat sister say, "Dad?" Dodging aflame path killer phallus, host sister say, "You're in *jail*?"

Same then, teeth operative me spread wide, legs spring, jawbone this agent snap shut, find purchase around flaming missile, *snatch-catch*, perfect Biting Bulldog. Crush renegade phallus. Molars render no longer threat.

All present strike together palms. Raucous cacophony applause. Attempt strike palms upon scapular this agent.

Saliva operative me flavored solder, scent cat sister some many night effort for construct device. Taste sweat of host sister labor. So wasted effort. Sour tang of guilt. Expectorate this agent masticated remnants scorched rocket.

Professor foot, shoe prodding smolder remains invention, say, "Thank God that didn't happen *inside* of someone . . ."

Awards top honor upon this agent. Hero of this today. Hero of Model United Nation. Hero of local science fair.

Total vast assemblage mounting verbal cheer. United of single voice, chant, "Pygmy!" Chant, "Pygmy!" Chant, "Pygmy!"

Quote, "On every side, the slug humanitarianism leaves its slimy trail, obscuring the function of intelligence and atrophying emotion."

Gazing ruin former menacing phallus, yelling at telephone, sister say, "But, Dad, why'd they *arrest* you?"

Same now marking most major strategic victory operative me—lauded vociferous by all, phallus conquered, competition project sabotaged—this exact now, host sister begin wail at telephone. Eye stealth cat sister commence copious bleed water.

Dispatch
Thirtieth

Begins here thirtieth account of operative me, agent number 67, upon return religion propaganda distribution outlet of city ███████. Seated among throng many citizen, vacuous lazy multitude citizen state ███████. Philosophically lax, morally despicable, culturally exhausted membership congregation religious community ███████. On occasion disposal cadaver devil Tony for nourish soil denizens.

Snake nest. American den of evil. Hive of corruption.

Casket containing devil staged position, same shrine location as casket of clear-yellow bully. Same location previous casket gun-shot delegate Zaire, delegate East Timor, Egypt, Brazil.

Open of ceremony, string embedded all paraffin cylinder, strings inflamed. Space perfumed genitals lush plant life. Statue man still dead, plaster bleeding red paint. Mounting altar of worship shrine, crippled zombie, stumbling ancient skeleton Doris Lilly. Hunched beside casket packaging mortal remains, decaying devil Tony, esteemed Miss Lilly say, cough thunder of phlegm noise upon microphone, say, "Due to the absence of our lay minister, Donald Cedar..." Say, "I've been asked to say a few words in regard to the tragic passing of Reverend Anthony..."

Host father Don Cedar, vast breathing cow, this today absent.

Twitching claws chicken mother, talons shred wadded facial tissue infinite bits. Host mother scented double extra dosed Xanax, perspiring abundant, pelvis no humming battery missile. Loins hollow of plastic vibration missile.

For official record, this today skills operative me having erased two American vermin, deleted two corrupt parasite—school gunner with pedophile. Yet aware no sensation fed. Discern no fulfillment mission. No satisfied such slaughter, instead solely aware such numerous more vermin to murder. Infinite quest such numbers for extermination, if perhaps no possible.

Additional seated bench of shrine, cat sister, pig brother.

Present operative Magda, hands of that agent hovering around hidden fetus.

Amidst present congregation mourners, female parentage Trevor Stonefield.

Doddering skeleton Doris Lilly deliver eulogy. Leaking eyeball gaping round, suffer such anguish. Such grieve. Explain devil Tony discovered strewn, fatal corpse fallen surprise casualty cerebral hemorrhage. Corpse chilled on account heart muscle so long time no contracted. Located beneath plaster foot, proof remain evident: atop carpet twin tiny stain blood leakage out devil ears canal.

Eulogy no mention inner bikini pants operative Magda, stained blood, seed, neurotoxin. Abandoned this agent, inner pants frozen within death spasm fingers devil Tony. Cotton fabric soiled, so fixed this agent no able retrieve. Forced abandon during feet operative me retreat.

In greater afraid . . . within thinking machine operative me, this agent ponder if entire being operative me pitted for destroy American, annihilate homosexual, crackpot Methodist religion, Lutheran and Baptist cult, extinguish all decadent bourgeoisie—subsequent successful total such destruction: Render this agent obsolete? Of no worth?

If possessing no vile enemy—will operative me cease also exist?

Seated for witness burial rite devil Tony, cat sister whisper, say, "My dad had some contract to invent something," say host sister. "It was some new caramel vanilla fudge flavor for some Starbucks-kind of franchised global coffee hut." Say, "The taste was supposed to be irresistible..."

Reason why host father, Don Cedar, seized in custody police. Victim military-industrial complex joined action corporate food conspiracy.

Lingering, amidst contents thinking machine operative me, discern perhaps this agent caught, also contained trap. Compelled nurture and preserve dreaded American enemy, if solely for provide target hatred operative me. Hatred homeland state operative me. Must this agent forever ensure supply American vermin for ensure ongoing mission to make extinct?

Echoing within skull operative me, no certain which more breed terror: Preserve enemy. Or, successful resolve single driving purpose, energy of vast hatred, lifetime vocation this agent.

Cat sister seated adjacent bench, scented solder, reeking black smoke issued exploding killer phallus, melted attacking phallus. Cat sister say, "What happened was this reverse Louis Pasteur deal." Say, whisper say during burial rites, say, "Their banana-caramel-nut deal got contaminated." Say, "It grew this *superdeadly* mold..."

Much venerated mummy, decayed carcass Doris Lilly move parrot mouth, droning. Withered hand mop seepage of clouded cataract eyeball.

Whisper cat sister explain, artificial flavoring tainted bacterium, bloom fungus extreme toxic spore, original source neurotoxin deemed too deadly except permanent deep storage, frozen. No utilized flavoring franchised coffee beverage. Despite so flavorful, banana-caramel-nut essence deemed threat all humanity, required top-priority secured secret vault.

This now, same now during sister whisper, mummy Doris Lilly void nasal mucus out nostril so cling cupped tissue. Fill microphone terrible sound. Wipe face of sopping tissue, say, "At this time, I invite everyone who loved our beloved reverend to stand and come forward..." Say, "To make your last farewells..."

For official record, no citizen straighten legs for make stance.

Operative Magda cast eyeball upon this agent. Cat sister cast eye upon Magda.

Duration now, then now, then now, many lasting now, no citizen make stance. All retain seated.

According cat sister, whisper, recent audit, neurotoxin no accounted for. Sole clue, security record dictating Don Cedar frequent foray during nighttime. Violated facility night of today neurotoxin vanished. Upon toxin no longer resident, legal authority seize host father suspicion theft. Maximum incarcerate pending investigate.

Final operative Magda make straight legs. Emerge out end of bench. Legs Magda take stride routed central aisle, several stride so approaching casket decomposed devil.

Same now, female parentage clear-yellow bully, eye cast upon this agent. Married partner of arrested male Stonefield, eye fixated upon face operative me. Clenched hand female Stonefield, pinched between fingers sheet white-colored paper. Snared within clutches, white paper envelope.

Same now pig brother emerge out bench one side shrine aisle. That now, emerge female parentage Trevor out opposite bench entering central aisle. Two citizen meeting. Female say secret message, head tipped almost to contact hearing ear of pig dog brother. Host brother twisted ear so listen, hand pig brother rise so accept envelope, white envelope relinquished female finger.

Next then, both citizen stride aisle. Ranked among throng awaiting for pay last respects to packaged carcass.

Ranting skeleton Doris Lilly, trembling mask dead skin, wadded leather mask, say, "I feel certain our cherished recently departed reverend would agree when I say..." Say, "'Words build bridges into unexplored regions.'"

Eyes historic venerated madam fixed atop face operative me. Withered eye matched eye this agent.

Awaiting visit casket, pig dog brother eviscerate white paper envelope, ogle letter sheet folded therein. Host brother reading letter.

Whisper cat sister protest, say, "He's my *dad.*" Say, "And pretty quick he's going to be *your* dad, too." Say, "We can't just let him rot in *jail.*"

Twisted mouth outlined red wax, pushed into microphone, repeat say Doris Lilly, ancient withered cadaver say, "'Words...build...bridges...into...unexplored...regions...'"

Exact quote maniac chieftain, admirable guide Adolf Hitler.

Dispatch
Thirty-first

Begins here thirty-first account of operative me, agent number 67, recall training session. On passed occasion practice physical education, ministry of health, city ███████. Conducting resistance training Romanian dead lifts, Bulgarian split squats, ███████, overhead press. Under observation, direct report revered director master health administrator ███████.

Depict here standard studio strength training, cluttered infinite racks graduated iron metal weights. Fixed bars boasting fifty-pound, hundred-pound, two-hundred-pound resistance. Level bench equipped scaffold allowing press, military press, bend-over rowing. Concrete constructed all floor and wall. Clang numerous iron weight striking floor. Clank weight impacting other weight.

Grunting operative Bokara during heave weights. Grunt bellow misery such effort Otto. Gasp groan exertion operative Metro.

Lain flat atop surface bench, arms operative me, abductor muscles this agent resistance training burdened numerous hundreds pounds oppression. Repeated lift-lower metal units subject massive pull gravity, clanking disks of cast iron mounted either end sturdy bar. Crushing so burdened.

For official record, partnered during resistance training operative Magda. During bench press operative me, Magda stance astride face this agent, ready so to seize crushing bar burdened infinite weights at failure arms operative me. Regal crotch Magda looming above nose this agent, operative me rise, lower, rise, lower burdened metal bar, expanding pectoral muscle in noble service glorious state.

Expand, contract chest of this agent, during Magda say, trumpet encourage, say, "Throw aside shackles, comrade." Say, "No endure silly weasel." Say, "Permit no oppression Western nations crushing citizen skull."

Bones operative me, muscles creak, joints pop. Tendon tremble under pain. Arms this agent heaving shivers, vibrate so ready fail. Rise burden. Lower burden. Breath trapped within rib cage. Face skin heated heavy blood glow.

Magda say, hiss say, "Suffer, slave bitch." Say, "Squirm under boot heel American domination!" Shout say, "Struggle so resist American control, weak puppet!"

Operative Magda leaning own weight upon cast-iron plates skewered exercise bar, Magda say, "Suffer underfoot crushing pressure United State media, industry of degradation!" Pelvic floor of that agent settling so smother across nose operative me, Magda drive weight down to collapse sternum this agent, Magda shouting say, "Grinding gears Western colonial tyranny, masticating millstone imperialism..." Shout say, "Comrade!" Shout, "American hunger ravenous for macerate all global citizen!"

Laboring this agent for survive, resist knotted muscle Magda arm. Skull operative me pinched between thick, heavily scented, massive thighs, hard gluteal muscles operative Magda.

This agent no able breathe.

Both vast hypertrophy muscle arm of Magda, thick driving iron so collapse thorax operative me.

"Prepare, comrade," say Magda. Say, "For become crushed beneath looming wheel ruthless Western ideology."

Next then, door training chamber swing so no healed within wall. Reveal much revered director master health administrator, boot planted wide apart, fist resting atop iliac crest each hip bone. Visage casting eye upon all operative.

For official record, according rule, all present Tibor, Magda, Vaky, say in single voice unison, "Greetings, esteemed most revered director." Operative Mang, Chernok, Tanek in unite voice say, "Accept, please, our gratitude for the wisdom you impart."

Pinned beneath weighted bar, compressed rib cage of this agent, voice operative me say, croak, "Accept, please..." Heart muscle rupturing underneath such pressure. Lung collapsed such burden, say whisper, "...for the wisdom you impart."

Director master bow head.

Operative all bow head.

Director master quote ample monarch, capacious tutor Adolf Hitler, say, "'Hate is more lasting than dislike.'"

Boots stride small parade, polished black parade so attain center of chamber. Stance at focus all operative. Chest plated thick, victorious legacy many awarded medals. Director master appareled uniform draped epaulets heavy cords much gold braid. Shoulders sway gold fringe. Director hand vanish into chest of tunic, emerge bearing thick sheaf many paper.

Paper revealed as glossy photo. Vast collection numerous such photo.

Same current now, burly arms operative Magda, bulging muscles rescue this agent. Lift burden weighted bar. Deposit aloft safety rack.

Vision operative me swimming with stars. Raving galaxy stars. Deltoids, triceps, pectoral muscle this agent rendered flimsy rubber. Limbs remaindered slack with fatigue.

Gesture director master, requiring all present for gather. All operative approach.

Next now, top best esteemed director distribute glossy photo arrayed surface concrete floor. Commence pave floor using many such photographs. Creating expansive mosaic, expanding ever more large, growing area until require operative stride backward so allow space. Disburse more photograph, always more photograph.

For official record, depicted every such image: Meat. Blood. Bone. Masticated macerated shredded skin fat sinew tissue dripping. Wrung pale strands. Puddled thick ketchup of gore. Battered tissues. Pulp pooling red juice. Shard shattered bone.

Pictures growing so occupy entire vision: Mutilated debris. Shredded flesh sponge sopping blood. Mangled jumble crumble studded much bone. Brilliant white color bone. Wadded skin. Tattered skin. Mess twisted gray meatloaf former thinking machine. Blasted spatter, scarlet splash.

Growing carpet such photograph spread until nearly fill chamber. Tide photo edge more large. Swelling red. Glossy wet shine. Blood photo flood floor so require all operative stride backward, heels trapped against concrete wall. Tibor, Magda, Oleg, all operative wedged between vast sea bloody meat, shoulders pinned against chilled concrete wall.

"Attention, young comrades," say director master. Say, "Examine much closely this exhibition."

Arrayed, yawning before all: Mixed collage, meadow montage commingled dead. No discernible human face. Solely wide pool pulped meat.

"Honored here," say director master, "witness final earthly fate unfortunate parentage..."

Honored family this agent: result American terrorist bomb. Evidence atrocity explosion.

No face. No survive. Burst violent pain, all family erased. So violent deleted.

Beloved parentage operative me: martyrs to American prejudice. Sacrificed for imperial aspiration depraved United State peoples.

So typical of America—land selling breakfast cereal with pistol buried in package as premium. No surprise, immoral nation host slashing razor death wrestling cage competitions. Rally monstrous truck.

Image such red blood paint all operative into concrete corner.

Quote, "Hate is more lasting than dislike."

Next then, director master hand delve within tunic. Emerge fingers clutching cardboard folder, margin folder printed, "Operation Havoc."

Dispatch
Thirty-second

Begins here thirty-second account of operative me, agent number 67, seated amid sleeping vault of host sister. This today, following daily instruction ███████ High School. During host mother sojourn so interrogate confined host father at ██████ Federal Building. During host brother engaged practice sport ███████.

This today, no happy tiny tremble shiver house. No happiness missile craft shiver within liquid depths host mother basement. No battery shaking own innards. For official record, residence host family Cedar vacant but for stealth cat sister and this agent.

Current now, sister perch adjacent work surface, gripping solder iron. Conduct for explore dead corpse of killer science fair phallus. Scraping aside melted plastic, carbon black charred circuitry. Investigate possible reason catastrophic malfunction such phallus endangering all bystander. Curving sinew spiraling tail white smoke rise out tip solder iron, smoke drawing pattern in air.

Sister analyze possible why prized project rejected top award local science fair. Killer phallus autopsy.

Host sister drip and draw in melted lead, breathing snake tail of smoke. Say, "Well, Pygmy..." No look eye except upon postmortem phallus, say, "Maybe the whole world loves you, but I sure don't."

Ear of operative me, steady consume sister word, only no able decipher. This agent sit balanced edge on host sister bed, mattress pile with blanket, many animals of brown weave. Animal all smile. Brown animal clench string bound to floating bladder inflated helium.

Mouths of operative me, say, "Define?"

Silly animal.

Cat sister squint eye at heat, molten solder liquid lead atop work surface, say, "You messed with my project, didn't you?"

In secret, inner voice operative me recite periodic table, say, *Aluminum, antimony, angora . . .*

Veiled within smoke, haloed and misted pale smoke of hot metal, sister face say, "You turned traitor on me." Say, "When I trained you as a spy . . ." Wielding glowing hot wand, sister face say nothing. Silent. Nose vent metal smoke. Acrid. Mouth say, "And you sabotaged my science fair project."

This agent within skull reciting, *Argon, arsenic, Ann Arbor . . .*

Next now, in breathe snaking white smoke, cat sister say nothing. No say anything. Await response.

"Imperative," say this agent, aloud say, "Sister must no attend finals National Science Fair." Say, "Imperiled there." Say, "Much total dangerous."

Face tilted within floating path, curve corkscrew white threads smoke, host sister say, "Why should I believe you now?" Say, "All you ever do is tell lies."

Quote this agent glorious revolutionary, heroic figurehead Eugene Debs, say, "'Progress is born of agitation. It is agitation or stagnation.'"

Eye blink against white smoke, cat sister say, "Real smarts begin when you quit quoting other people . . ."

Thinking machine operative me recite, *Zinc, zirconium, Zoloft . . .*

This agent request source such profound statement.

"Who am I *quoting*?" say cat sister. Bunch shoulders at own ears, making shrugged, say, "I guess I'm quoting myself..."

Hand of this agent rise, all finger made straight as for pledge. Lips operative me say, "Team Cedar?"

Sister no make slap hands. Next then, host cat sister parry, thrust burning point of soldering iron, brandish so threaten contact this agent with sharpen fire-color tip. Burning heat. So menacing, host sister say, "Now get the fuck out of my room."

Dispatch
Thirty-third

Begins here thirty-third account of operative me, agent number 67, upon foray retail outlet Wal-Mart for purchase provisions National Science Fair. Fresh inner pants, paste of teeth, hair comb, supplies required purpose of travel airplane flight ███████. Journey so housed corrupt luxury hotel ███████. Hatch wide distribution deadly neurotoxin ███████, instant kill American millions, likely in addition Tibor, Mang, Ling, all fellow operative—including operative me. Likely additional martyr Magda, burdened with fetus. Accomplish lifetime mission Operation Havoc.

Solely no murder cat sister, host sister. Best beloved despite recent loathing that sister for this agent. Operative me shall die same manner as Trevor Stonefield—adoring only no adored.

Alone. No beloved. Appareled fresh inner pants.

Magic quiet door go sideways, disappear inside wall to open path from outside. Doors slide gone until reveal inside stand old slave woman appareled with red tunic, Doris Lilly. Ancient sentinel rest gray cloud eye on operative me, roll eye from hair and down this agent, say, voice like old parrot, say, "Welcome to Wal-Mart." Say, *"Comrade."*

Inquires this agent, face operative me designed into pleasing eye contact. This agent say, "Much venerate ancient mother... where sold here sterile inner—"

Next now, halt. Thinking machine operative me fixed upon word *comrade.*

Face of ancient mummify bound in dying skin, clouded eye only look, no blink.

Same now, voice say, "Hey, Pyg man." From elsewhere nearby, male voice say, "Can I talk to you?"

Ancient parrot, sag skin jump with smile. Edge smear of red wax slice open as mouth, wax smile spread so reveal prosthetic teeth, say, "Good luck at the National Science Fair..."

Male voice revealed as pig dog brother. On breath, the stink of Ritalin. The pollution stench of model airplane adhesive and frequent masturbations. Host brother brandish sheet white paper, sheet revealed as envelope. Fingers pig dog pluck envelope so open, extract paper colored white. Standard-size letter. Say, "You got a minute?"

Envelope delivered hand of female Stonefield, amid burial rites devil Tony.

Hand operative me aware folded newsprint photograph within trouser this agent. Aware vial neurotoxin purloined office of arrested host father. Allowing single inhale, able murder host brother. Murder Doris Lilly. Resolve all mysteries and possible conflict.

Aware molar tooth this agent, filled hollow with deadly cyanide. Forever so able resolve this agent utilizing single bite.

En route, approached operative Tibor, that agent bestowing thick stack, vast quantity paper American currency upon operative me. Serious mass load many notes one, five, twenty-dollar bills.

For official record, allow pig dog brother lead this agent making small parade. Stride passing location clear-yellow bully brutalize host brother. Stride past table numerous shoe for purchase. Tennis shoe, track shoe, bowling shoe. Wrestling shoe. Basketball shoe. Cross-training shoe. Arriving shelves burdened cologne of Listerine, host brother halt, make eyes sideways one direction, sideways other direction. No fellow citizen present as witness.

Next then, happen upon former gentleman delegate Tanzania, occasion catalyst vast smile, delegate say, "Pyg-ster!" Say, "Hey, good buddy!"

Next then, stumble upon Madam Butter Bags. Esteemed madam bat flirt eye, say squeal, "Pygmy!" Say, "*Wow* about that science fair thing!"

Upon occasion alone, isolated amid empty aisle accompanied solely host brother, hands host brother open paper sheet. Fingers vibrating. Trembling. Voice of pig dog in additional trembling, say, "I need to read you something Mrs. Stonefield gave me..."

In response this agent could offer instruct pig brother, *paw-raw*, pounce Clawing Cougar.

Eyes pig dog darting evasive, no connecting eyes this agent. English alphabet letters, written by hand alongside of envelope, written, "For Pygmy."

Negotiate could be operative me train host brother, *slash-crash*, execute perfect exact Tearing Tiger.

That now, approached operative Tanek for deliver that agent large volume, serious bulk additional American monetary notes.

Pig brother eyes fixed upon letter sheet, say, read say, "'Dear Pygmy...'"

This agent offer, could be teach brother, *claw-craw*, Pawing Panther. After able instant quick kill all enemy.

"'Dear Pygmy,'" repeat say host brother, "'Probably I shouldn't feel embarrassed, because if you're reading my letter then I've got to be dead.'"

In secret thinking machine operative me, no voice reciting, *Nickel, niobium, Naughahyde*...

Read say out letter, host brother say, "'That's probably for the best.'"

Within skull reciting, *Fermium, fluorine, Formica . . .*

Read say, "'Better to be dead, I figure, than alive and knowing what I can't have. You know?'" Read say, "'Maybe it's better just living the way you figure life is when you're a kid. Before you get too smart.'"

Ultimate million reflections this agent, pig dog brother, striding past everything new with shine. Polished plastic. Tight stretches vinyl. Everything American begging for take home.

Pig brother say off paper, "'If I could go back to before you and me in the bathroom, definitely probably I'd jump at the chance. Only problem is, I can't.'" Read say, "'If you won't share my life with me, maybe you'll share my death.'"

Eye cast upon letter, read say, "'Sorry about tomorrow at the United Nations, how I'm tricking you to kill me.'" Read say, "'You made me somebody new. That's plenty.'" Read say, "'Thank you.'"

In closing, paper written, "Love." Written, "Trevor Stonefield."

Fingers operative me aware vial tucked within trouser, toxin. Within skull reciting prayer of benevolent hero, altruist savior Mao Tse-tung, say, *"If you have to shit, shit! If you have to fart, fart! You will feel much better for it."*

"That money you gave me at Wal-Mart," say pig brother, say, "it smelled like ass . . ." Say, "How'd that happen?"

From distant, far terminus aisle, solely witness aged skeleton Doris Lilly. Clouded eye observe, no blink. Next now, menacing wrinkled head tilt, nod, repeat to make head meaning "yes." Feet ominous cadaver make exit, wander so no more present, eclipsed behind many absurd breakfast food, heaped expiring foodstuffs.

Dying objects. Dying buyers. Desperate how sad.

Arriving that then, operative Chernok, imparting generous portion, much heavy funds cash of American legal tender. Paper bills printed portraits presidents Lincoln, Jackson, Washington.

Quote, "If you have to shit, shit! If you have to fart, fart! You will feel much better for it."

Hands operative me delve more deep trouser, fingers clutch glass vial. Extract so able present for pig dog. Voice of this agent, pitched casual, explain how vial as Listerine: effective cologne for driving all the fine ladies wild. Display vial so most appealing. Announce, here invented such super-mega-effective Spanish fly as pig brother requested. Rise elevate vial fatal toxin, hand making ever more close host brother face.

Dispatch
Thirty-fourth

Begins here thirty-fourth account of operative me, agent number 67, on departure Midwestern American airport greater ██████ area. Flight ██████. Date ██████. Destination competition finals National Science Fair, located city of Washington, District of Columbia, national seat most hated American nation.

For purpose execute climax Operation Havoc.

Fellow operatives present interior airport, operative Tibor, operative Magda, operative Ling. All, Sheena, Bokara, Chernok, Mang. Otto and Oleg.

Present for departure this agent, solely host mother Cedar. Scrawny chicken mother, beak face irritated much red color, caused recent too copious eye bleeding water. Host father: detained custody federal police. Host pig brother: missing. Host cat sister: Hating guts operative me.

Aged alive cadaver Doris Lilly, present for accompany as chaperone along science fair journey.

Host mother, chicken claws wring facial tissue at beak. Twist tissue so saturated eye water, say, "Have a good trip..." Say, "We'll miss you..." Chicken frame shaken with heaving sob, blood glow flood face red.

Within skull, this agent reciting, *Manganese, Mouseketeer, Modesto...*

Host mother racked violent sobs. Mopping floodwater of face.

Secret voice operative me, reciting, *Xenon, Ex-Lax, Xanax*...

Chicken mother wipe saturated face skin. Loud inhale nostrils loaded infinite mucus. Repeat breathe inward dense burden mucus. Issue terrible drowning voice, say, "Pygmy?" Say, "Do you remember how I said we'd make you into an American or die trying?"

Chicken mouth wane smile, brimming eyes, say, "Well, if you jumped the first plane back to your native homeland, I wouldn't blame you one little bit." Mauling moist tissue, say, "This family...our whole country is a total wreck."

Father arrested. Son missing. Sister betrayed. Mother weeping.

Blink watery eye, swipe dripping beak, host mother say, "I would understand completely if you didn't want to be adopted, I mean..." Shoulders heave, quaking. Chicken elbows pinned at each side. Mother say, "Everything is just so messed up right now."

Both twitching limbs host mother fling so embrace this agent. Grapple torso operative me, pressuring head of this agent between host mother mammary glands. Dampening hair operative me much mother eye water. Sounding contractions, *beat-beat, beat-beat, beat-beat*, regular systematic convulsions mother heart muscle into ear of this agent.

Heart pulse battling thinking machine, recitation basic chemical elements, *Neon, nylon, Nashville*...

Next then chaperone Doris Lilly approach, stumbling stride arrive wrinkled mummy, waxen face say, "Sorry, dears, but it's time we caught our flight..."

Assembled crowd cheering students, chanting single voice, "Pygmy!" Chanting, "Pygmy!" Cheering, "Pygmy!"

Clutches Doris Lilly pinch shoulder operative me, parrot finger clench clavicle bone so peel this agent away host mother. Steer so this agent directed path of boarding aircraft. Making ancient hand to wave upon retreating host mother. Gesturing farewell, Doris Lilly say, "'Afterwards you rue the fact that you've been so kind.'"

For official record . . . no possible.

Withered madam precise quote furious leader, ruthless general Adolf Hitler.

Black tunic appareled this agent, "Property of Jesus," printed eye water abandoned host mother.

Host mother stoop until face level with face operative me. Mother purse lips of face, offer gesture to contact lips against face skin of this agent in expression so demonstrate affection.

Quote, "Afterwards you rue the fact that you've been so kind."

In opposition past history, infamous day separated from female parentage for vocational testing, feet operative me retreat from entry aircraft, make sprint, flee returned upon host mother. Accept proffered embrace. Pressure lips this agent against chicken mother face cheek, sodium chloride taste eye water. Pursed lips making gesture meaning affection.

Next then, exited for flight, mouth operative me flavored lingering salt of mother's great sorrow. Bound for infinite destruction.

Dispatch
Thirty-fifth

Begins here, today of this agent's noble demise.

For official record, squander final dawn housed luxury hotel ████████. Observe television viewing appliance, program ████████. Witness American president ████████ speak small announcement, likely by night of today president in addition deceased. Millions deceased. Careful hands operative me pack final preparation, steel metal canister approximate size can for refuse. In actual, formerly galvanized can housing garbage. Stenciled encircling exterior can, English letter words: "Peace Machine." Executed utilizing Day-Glo pink-color paint. Garnished many depictions daisy plant, singing bluebird trilling musical note. Decorated plethora arched rainbow. Scripted more-small letters, labeled "Path to Permanent Global Peace."

Invention so eradicate every strife within single generation humanity. Craft world happy sunshine peace. Beneficent lovely flower peace.

Into mirror of toilet room, this agent offer face shining facsimile expression smile. Practice briefly repeating lips operative me making multiple such false smile.

Next then, set timing device of science fair project. Adjust so explode amid afternoon height of exhibition, surrounded most numerous crowd. Activate this agent trigger of exploding mechanism. Abrade teeth operative me using paste of tooth. Organize head hair using comb. Apparel this agent placing legs through holes sterile inner pants. Doff white blouse associated attendance worship shrine, bind neck operative me knotted silk banner. Make small parade, encumbered deadly machine, direction hotel elevator. Limbs operative me embracing can for carry, ear of this agent pressed to steel metal so listen quiet *tick-tick* of timing device, hidden within.

Such opposite pulse of mother heart muscle.

For official record, escorted by chaperone Doris Lilly, journey of taxi automobile destination vast assembly hall Smithsonian Institute. Enormous vaulted hall. Incorporated among infinite doomed fellow student. All clutching, carry project in transit. Forever muscles operative me tensioned for possible "Peace Machine" premature explode. Girded loins always for imminent die. Forever flooded perspiration until deadly gadget ensconced center exhibition space, surrounded multitudes venomous American vipers.

Secret, in nervous, this agent reciting whisper of elements, "Mercury, molybdenum, marijuana..."

All entire generation operatives present: Magda, Tibor, and Ling. Tanek, Chernok, and Sheena. Bokara, Oleg, and Otto. Vaky, Metro, and Mang. All staunched for await inevitable demise, beaming false expression smile. Engaging American baboons, invite for make a more close inspection "Peace Machine."

Many such oblivious United State citizen approach this agent, inquire if actually Pygmy of school rescue fame. Reverent Pygmy, renowned for spoiled slaughter delegates. Such curious onlookers queue for attain autographed paper marked this agent. Cluster dense surrounding faint *tick-tick* death machine.

Chaperone Doris Lilly, red wax lips beaming. Assembled operatives beaming.

This today, culmination whole lifetime. Purpose determined best service to state.

Infiltrate hive, den, pit American predators. Murder vile overlords.

Revenge savage terrorist slaughter parentage operative me.

For ignore memory cat sister, thinking machine operative me recite, *Strontium, sulfur, spandex...*

Recite, *Lithium, Librium, latex...*

Recite, *Radium, radon, Rachael Stodard...*

Hand crafting word *Pygmy* atop papers. Hand agitating offered hands American strangers.

Next now, voice say, "Hey." Female voice. Face of host sister.

Embedded among crowd American vermin for assassinate—cat sister. This now—sister present self. Leering face of half smile, host sister say, "You fucked up my science project..." Say, "Now I'm here to return the favor."

Strident voice operative me, making screech say, insist best top important cat sister flee this venue. Hurry flee this instant. Next whisper, control voice, say imminent soon detonate "Peace Machine," raining death down upon all in attendance.

Cat sister merely rotate skull one direction, rotate skull opposite direction, repeat to make head meaning "no."

For official record, this agent launched amid personal vast crisis. Most happy enough for kill infinite random American swine, grasping, jostling, crowds American rodents. Avenge parentage operative me...Erase influence vile United State culture corrupting global villagers...Delete starving American citizen appetite consuming all world resources...

Solely no able include murder glorious cat sister.

Eyes all fellow operatives cast upon this tableau. Suspicious apparent scenario.

Pitched whisper, voice operative me say, "Affectionate comrade." Say, "Required immediate exit this doomed city."

Explain this agent, contained vessel "Peace Machine" many fortunes paper American legal tender. Numerous weight pounds and kilograms monetary bills American money. Cash stolen out contribution plates community worship shrine. Vast fortune such currency wealth, compressed above miniature explosive charge. Upon impending now, almost arrived now, shall device explode showering all in attendance with windfall denominations mass quantity United State paper money.

Stealth sister merely look in return, no blink.

Explain this agent, on occasion device triggered, greedy capitalist citizens melee for gather filthy lucre. Million hundred hands grasp-snatch dirty currency.

Stealth sister remain looking, no blink.

According procedure required Operation Havoc, all such released money tainted neurotoxin. Catalyst ten days, trigger death of individuals exposed. No cure. No escape. Tainted money spent into circulation expected generate infinite additional more casualty. All present to die. All accepting such money—die. Toxic American money predicted spread until kill all capitalists.

Cat sister poised, brow muscle knotted in expression frustration. Roll eyeball, say, "So, you're telling me that you're a *terrorist* . . . ?"

No, this agent explain own self as operative promoting freedom native glorious homeland.

"Whatever," say host sister.

"It's not that I don't believe you," say host sister. Say, "But I'm still going to wreck your project." Next now, sister dive forward lunge. Delve hands so gripping refuse can of "Peace Machine." Wrestling for overturn vessel, attempt to fail execution death machine. Foil objective flying flurry killer money.

Same now, ancient skeleton Doris Lilly stride present. Stricken, withered corpse fingers grip own gray curls, yank so reveal scalp shaved of hair. Shining pate. Cadaver mouth expectorate prosthetic teeth so clatter across exhibition flooring. Waxed red lips curl, whole sinew frame assume stance hideous ninja assassin, posture top high battling arts warrior. Balance all muscle into striking position Giant Stork Death Kick. Scream attack challenge.

Same now, sister activate siren of rapes, create emitting earpierce screaming horn. Blinding loud so fill all location.

Wal-Mart slave Doris Lilly revealed as mole superoperative, buried secret agent for ensure success Operation Havoc. Bony skeleton looming power, poised so launch deadly fatal blow upon cat sister.

Feet operative me, flying elbows this agent, spring landing *sock-block*, Soaring Condor Double Strike maneuver, blocking fatal strike. This agent toppling superior talent superagent Doris Lilly. Body muscle operative me committing full treason. Betray own thinking machine this agent.

Instant quick then, Madam Cadaver spring returned to fighting stance. Reinforced also, flanked ready killing limbs operative Tibor. Backed slashing death kicks operative Mang. Chernok. Sheena. All agent ranked along superagent in opposition solely operative me.

Siren shrieking scream.

Launching then Flying Tree Squirrel *zoom-grab*, Flying Hyena *lash-pow*, Elephant Stomp *swish-bang*, Lashing Lynx *slash-scratch*. Atmosphere blurred multitude flashing fist, infinite bashing foot. Vast vaulted assembly hall filled crowded screams all onlooker. Great rush for escape turmoil tumult gouging fingers, biting teeth.

Final now all operative converged destroy this agent, that now cat sister delve hand into own luggage purse, extract infamous killer attack phallus. During circle of operatives encroaching for kill, edging more close, host sister say, "Let's hope my mom didn't swipe the batteries." Finger slide activate dildo switch, say sister, "And let's *really* hope I didn't totally *repair* this sucker..."

Edging more close, ranked wall of killer assassins stance ready for execute Cobra One-Strike No-Blood. For land Leaping Kangaroo Punch Escape. For render Barracuda Deadly Eye Gouge.

Jumping so legs make, *pow-pow*, Tearing Tiger, operative Tibor quote keen visionary, astute author D. H. Lawrence, say, "'They want an outward system of nullity, which they call peace and goodwill, so that in their own souls they can be independent little gods.'"

Crafting counteract, elbows operative me launch, *rip-scrape*, Clawing Cougar, during quote brilliant philosopher, learned professor Fidel Castro, this agent say, "'Men do not shape destiny. Destiny produces the man for the hour.'"

Throwing, *sock-pow*, Punching Panda, operative Mang quote revered Fidel Castro, say, "'A revolution is a struggle between the future and the past.'"

Hitting, *blam-wham*, Striking Cobra Quick Kill maneuver, operative Chernok quote respected Friedrich Nietzsche, say, "'One must still have chaos in oneself to be able to give birth to a dancing star.'"

Returning, *sock-block*, Flying Eagle maneuver, this agent

quote acclaimed Fidel Castro, say, "'Condemn me. It does not matter. History will absolve me.'"

Same current now, deadly phallus commence tremble. Pink phallus deepening more dark pink. Tinting red. Shivering phallus initial small wobble. Leap from cat sister hand. Trailing spiral black smoke, ricochet off floor. Midair thrashing, killer phallus spray heated molten plastic every all direction upon hostile operative. Suppress attack. Ignited fragments plastic spattering operative Tanek. Blinding operative Bokara. Torching head hair operative Sheena. Plumes huge flame, strong stink.

Siren of rapes always howl. Echo loud filling vast institute of Smithsonian.

Operative Magda hesitate, hold back from such array hazardous contacts.

Bursting battlefront of flying fire phallus, Madam Cadaver throw wild Lashing Lion, *rip-roar*, clubbing skull of this agent. Immediate capable and prepared for execute this seditious operative me. Create fulfillment Operation Havoc.

That then, voice say, "Pygmy, my man!" Male voice. Resurrected pig dog brother.

Leaping amid fray, host brother assume defensive stance, say, "You taught me too much, little man." Say, "I got out of those ropes with no trouble..." Facing approach murderous cadaver, pig brother say, "What do you suggest?" Making steely eye, say, "Punching Panda or Lunging Lynx?"

Killer phallus providing aerial cover, bombing hot plastic. Obscuring conflict with black smoke screen. Choking soot and smut.

This agent stunned subsequent Lashing Lion impact skull.

Cat sister prepared disarm canister packed ready for burst legal tender.

On occasion American mob witness attack on this agent, mob riot in defense. United State citizen swarm, swamp, overwhelm Tibor, Chernok. Subdue Mang, Ling, Oleg. No longer passive, vast crowd surge for rescue operative me. Arriving as salvation this agent, sheer numerous hordes American citizen clumsy punch, push, grab so surmount actions operative Otto, Vaky, Tanek.

Madam Doris Lilly burst tension of accumulated career training, lifetime supermole agent, entire limbs rocketing for inflict, *punch-crunch*, fatal Monkey Mash upon all.

Same then, slow motion, operative Magda launch self in defense of pig dog brother. Magda leaping midair. Magda and brother collide simultaneous, blasting skull Doris Lilly. Inflict coma upon evil agent thinking machine. Throwing no conscious superagent to heap upon floor. Crumpled agent adjacent discarded own prosthetic teeth. Adjacent discarded scalp of gray curls. Rage subjugated.

Within that now most greatest victory. Magda and pig dog, beaming. Sputtering phallus routing attack fellow agents. American forces delivering rescue. Cat sister kneel so minister wounded operative me.

That same current now, dreaded "Peace Machine" explode.

Flickering American riches paper money showering, snowing blizzard, rain down so engulf all.

Dispatch
Thirty-sixth

Begins here thirty-sixth account of operative me, agent number 67, recalling former practice American language studies. Classroom warren deep interior ███████ building. Capital city ████████ of best top glorious homeland ████████. For official record, repeat recounting here formative history of operative me.

For reinforce early lesson training of operative me.

Benevolent much respected language instructor, making stance at focus all operative, say, "Hep cat." Say, "Cat's meow." Say, "Cat's pajamas."

Repeat say all operative, "Hep cat. Cat's meow. Cat's pajamas."

Learned, best-meaning instructor say, "Rumble seat."

All student say, "Rumble seat."

All learn so able repeat, "Soda pop. Twenty-three skidoo. Monkey wrench. Grease monkey. Raccoon coat."

Seated desks, hands folded, eyes cast forward, all operative repeat say, "Heavens to Betsy." Say, "Greased lightning." Say, "Moxie." Say, "Bluebird of happiness."

As affirmation correct usage current modern American language, honored instructor say, "Now you're cooking with gas!"

Same manner all operatives studied so learn repeat, say, "Workers' paradise." Say, "Heartless postcolonial multinational corporation."

Taught say, "Venomous vipers of capitalist imperial United States."

Taught memorize, implant within thinking machine, "Oppressive degenerate Western culture."

Implanted quote from celebrated author, infamous sodomite Oscar Wilde, say, "It is through disobedience that progress has been made, through disobedience and through rebellion."

In truth, many such facts actual outdated.

Admitting here failure of this agent. Operative me, traitor guilty of committing treason. Operation Havoc rendered utter aborted. Total disappointed of no result.

Begins here resignation of this agent.

Much shame saddled with great humiliation, this agent hereby admitting defeat. No able sacrifice life for state. Instead, have ended former life of this agent for benefit of host sister. In retreat, this agent seeking political asylum, adoption host family. All charges against host father dropped. Host family Cedar restored. All operative unmasked, held federal custody pending full investigate. As per plan, exploded cargo of dollars... legal monetary notes burst toward sky... except neglected this agent to taint said currency deadly neurotoxin. With full intention, no poisoned money, already operative me so seduced by affection for American parasites. Instead, "Peace Machine" merely geyser cash money into space. Delight assembled crowd children and adults of National Science Fair. Create vast celebration.

Quote, "It is through disobedience that progress has been made, through disobedience and through rebellion."

Go, Team Cedar!

Therefore tending here resignation operative me.

Confessed this agent responsible violent anal sodomy Trevor Stonefield.

Magda offspring due issue June seventeenth. Revealed of

DNA analysis, fathered pig dog brother. Perhaps intend wed. Perhaps no.

For official record, this agent rejects top deity as dictated by native state.

Please locate herewith enclosed molar tooth, extracted out mouth of operative me during visitation with United State doctor of teeth. Molar encasing hollow filled deadly cyanide, no longer of purpose for this agent.

Begins here new life of operative me.

Chuck Palahniuk's nine previous novels are the best-selling *Snuff, Rant, Haunted, Lullaby, Diary, Choke*—which has been made into a film by director Clark Gregg, starring Sam Rockwell and Anjelica Huston—*Survivor, Invisible Monsters*, and *Fight Club*, which was made into a film by director David Fincher. He is also the author of the nonfiction profile of Portland, Oregon, *Fugitives and Refugees*, published as part of the Crown Journeys series, and the nonfiction collection *Stranger Than Fiction*. He lives in the Pacific Northwest.

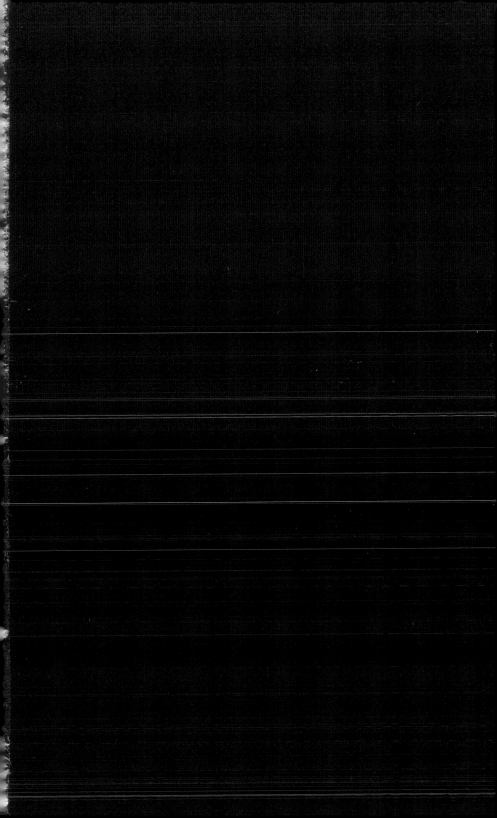